BIO-SAPIEN BOOK 3
Human Metamorphosis

Written by: Vlane Carter

Take a 360 video tour of Action Burger:

Action Burger's latest music video on youtube:

BIO-SAPIEN 101

JADEN'S HUMAN BODY BIO-ENGINEERED WITH ALIEN NANOTECHNOLOGY.

CONTROL YOUR BODY LIKE A STAR TREK ENTERPRISE SHIP.

CAPTAIN OF BIO-SAPIEN HOST: Jaden Marino. 5'10-6'1 155 LBS.

SECOND OFFICER IN CHARGE: AI – (AISCAN) Artificial Intelligent Synthetic Crystal Andromedian Nanobot.

CREW MEMBERS: NANODRONES (+1000 Quintillion) PCBOALF. – Prototype Carbon and Biochemical-based Organic Alien Life Forms; Also known as organic Nanobots.

LEFT ARM
– Atom Ripper Nanodrones embedded in skin; based on plasma fusion technology.

SPINAL CORD AND BACK
– Energy shield generating Nanodrones storage area. Brain controls RPM speed and direction of energy shield outside of body. Energy shield is base on plasma fusion technology and Neutrino energy. It retrieves most of its energy from replaced digestive system area.
– Magnetically charged Nanodrones enhances intervertebral disc of cartilage.

SKELETON
– Reconstructed Cancellous and Compact bones. Nanodrone webs of organic fiber proteins. 500 pounds per square inch of force needed to break a bone.

JOINTS
– Enhanced synovial joints around body. Magnetic energy between Nanodrones in joints makes the joints 10x stronger and flexible.

PENIS
– Multiple joints added to penal shaft for controllable directional curving.

BRAIN
– Rostral anterior cingulate cortex – Unknown signals transmitted when host feels pain or becomes angry.
– Instant on internal forward moving one layer energy shield, that extends around the skull.

EARS
– Enhanced equilibrium in inner ears. Nanodrones in ears communicate hi-speed with pro-gravity and magnetic Nanodrones in feet. They also communicate with anti-gravity Nanodrones in kidney/lower spine. Allows host to walk on walls or ceilings and feel as if he is walking on the ground.

ARMS
– Specially modified cells and tissue to accept high-energy forces.

RIGHT ARM
– Gravity shockwave Nanodrones embedded in skin.

MUSCLES
– Myostatin protein in muscles cells modified. MSTN gene decoded.
– On demand muscle strength equivalent to 2-4 HP.
– Musculoskeletal - Nanodrones enhances muscle fibers strength and coordinate with skeleton system.

RIGHT KIDNEY
– Internal tissue removed. Nanodrones doing the same job in the blood around body. Kidney replaced with quadrillions of Anti-gravity Nanodrones.

NERVOUS SYSTEM
– Nanodrones in brain bypasses chemical messages during Nanotime. They transmit hi-speed collective signals at 8000 feet per second to Nanodrones at nerve endings.

FEET
– Pro-gravity and magnetic Nanodrones; works directly with equilibrium in ears.

LEGS
– Enhanced muscles enables host to run and average between 20-30 Mph.
– Host can jump an unlimited height with anti-gravity Nanodrones support.

COPYRIGHT 2010 BY: VC IMAGINATION FACTORY
Illustration by: John Moriarty
Creative art director: Vlane Carter

"EVOLVE YOUR IMAGINATION"
WWW.BIO-SAPIEN.COM

4

BIO-SAPIEN 101
JADEN'S HUMAN BODY BIO-ENGINEERED WITH ALIEN NANOTECHNOLOGY.

CAPTAIN OF BIALIEN HOST: Jaden Marino.

SECOND OFFICER IN CHARGE: AI (AISCAN) Artificial Intelligent Synthetic Crystal Andromedian Nanobot.

ALIEN NANOTECHNOLOGY:

NANODRONES (+1000 Quintillion) PCBOALF – Prototype Carbon and Biochemical-based Organic Alien Life Forms. Also known as organic Nanobots. - Varies in size.
- Communicate in an atomic digital level 3 collective.
- Split into trillions of communities to perform millions of different duties in organic host.
- Nanodrones are loyal to the DNA of one host.

BRAIN
- 200 billion enhanced neurons.
- Neural code decoded. Neurotransmitters enhanced.
- Total brain usage 60-100%; up from 7-10% average Homosapien.
- New multitasking matrix area in the brain.
- RPM control area for forward and reverse energy shields.
- Artificial nicotine cigarette stimulation. Reconfigured Dopamine areas of the brain.
- Nanotime accelerates the communication speed in the brain. Time dilation reroutes to different parts of the brain. Nanodrones create artificial neurons, artificial synapses and axons. Host witnesses everything happening outside the body in slow motion. Nanotime ranges from 1x to 100x. 1x is the slowest speed and host can see a bullet approaching. Negative side is Nanotime puts a strain on brain and lasts only seconds, can lead to seizures.

LUNGS
- Nanodrones double lung capabilities. 30% more carbon dioxide leaves lungs from added oxygen breathing Nanodrones in skin.
- Instant on internal forward moving one layer energy shield, that extends through the rib cage and around heart.

DNA
- 10,000 compressed DNA memo groups in various locations around body.
- Encoded DNA. Built in anti-cloning prevention. DNA strips away when it leaves host.
- Modified DNA and RNA genetic code.
- Advanced protein folding.

BLOOD
- Reprogrammed white and red blood cells to accept Nanodrones.
- Artificial stem cells regeneration capacities. Rapid injury repair system.

COPYRIGHT 2010 BY: VC IMAGINATION FACTORY
Illustration by: John Moriarty
Creative art director: Vlane Carter

NANODRONE GOALS
- Remove and replace unnecessary body parts/organs.
- Evolve the BIO body to its maximum capabilities.
- Avoid alien metamorphosis. - Defend and protect host.
- Defrag and recalibrate the brain configuration for ultimate performance.
- Turn the human host into a powerful offensive and defensive weapon.
- Avoid technological singularity.

EYES
- Enhanced rods and cones behind eyes. 1 terapixel of resolution in each eye; zooming capabilities.
- Jaden's eyes command screen. Nanodrones reports, body's actions, offense and defense weapons, energy updates, statistics, energy shield RPM and navigation info.
- Nanoscanner images transmit to optic-nerve.

NANOSCANNERS
(Six Nanoscanners created from Nanodrones made for BIO host)
Autonomous alien molecules that vary in size. They transmit sound, smell, vision, and taste to host and help to do remote tasks. Nanoscanners also help to return gravity shockwave and atom ripper Nanodrones back to host.
- Programmable matter capabilities.

SKIN
- Artificial orbital hybridization web binds with skin cells; also known as Nanodrone nanotubing organic fibers.
- Self cleaning skin - Bacteria and dirt deposits around body pulls into skin and manually transported securely in blood stream by Nanodrones to throat area.
- Advanced photosynthesis in skin. Sunlight provides carbohydrate energy into blood stream. Host does not have to eat for days. When combined with water can produce oxygen.
- Light reflecting Metamaterial Nanodrones embedded around skin. Nanodrones can also reproduce air temperature molecules to match body heat signature.

STOMACH, SMALL AND LARGE INTESTINES
– Unnecessary organs; removed. Replaced with: Nanodrones energy storage areas, Atomic Solar Recharge fusion area and sub-atomic particles smashing areas.
- Nanodrones protect every outer cell in area from radiation energies.
- Nanodrones can do the same job the digestive system does in a fraction of an inch. Vitamins, minerals, salts, water, carbohydrates, amino acids from proteins, H2O, and fats from food, filter in seconds directly into the blood stream from the throat area. The rest redirects into the buttocks area for storage.
- Nanodrones redirect and duplicate chemical messages to let the brain know the organs are still there.

They pass through and scan any matter. They transmit sound, smell, vision and taste to host. They can also carry trillions of Nanodrones to do remote tasks.

- 100% filtered oxygen absorbed through pores and injected into the blood stream. Host can hold breath for 20-30 minutes. 30% carbon dioxide leaves hair follicles on head.

5

VC IMAGINATION FACTORY PRESENTS:

BIO-SAPIEN VOLUME I (BOOKS 1-6).

A SCI-FI, SPACE, ACTION, ADVENTURE & ROMANCE NOVEL

PROLOGUE

An average teenager Jaden Marino discovers a UFO landing one evening in upstate NY. The government is also looking for the mysterious UFO in the area. The government eventually follows him to it while trying to kill him. He hides inside of the advanced nanotechnology UFO while the government tries to take it away to Area 51 on a trailer. His mind goes into a comatose state and he has an out-of-the-body experience. The spaceship translates his English language from his mind into its language, enabling him to control the UFO with his mind. As he tries to fly away, the government sends all of their best and top-secret aircraft to intercept this very advanced spacecraft. Jaden quickly learns what this spaceship is capable of and goes against the best pilots in an intense chase over NY. Eventually he leaves Earth and travels 2.1 million light-years into the Andromeda Galaxy. He learns of an advanced alien species called Andromedians, who are 70,000 years ahead of humans. The Andromedians are peaceful explorers and their thinking is very far ahead of our own.

Jaden comes back to Earth eighteen years later and is aware of an alien conspiracy that is about to take place on Earth. He tries to warn people, but everyone thinks he is crazy. They lock him up in a mental ward. Society, relationships, values and technology has changed on Earth. He has a microscopic artificial intelligence alien companion in his mind helping him along the way, called AI. His body begins developing its advanced alien nanotechnology weapons system to work on Earth. After the government and citizens do not listen, he tries to help the people he cares about while the government places him on a terrorist list and uses their full military forces to kill him. He goes against the government's future weapons, Motherdrone (a super computer that controls all UAV drone crafts), super exoskeleton soldiers, SWATbots, thermobaric weapons and himself. At the same time, a bad alien race, called Darclonians, are implementing their silent planned strike on humans. An energy knight is the Darclonians new powerful weapon that can manipulate dark energy. Unbelievable movie style action sequences throughout the book and an ending you won't stop talking about. Jaden Marino's adventure of a lifetime begins.

BIO-SAPIEN SERIES (Formally known as the BIAlien trilogy.)

VOL I PROFESSIONAL BOOK REVIEWS

NOTE: Book reviews are based on all six books to volume I series.

"Science fiction fans unite! If the title doesn't say it all, I don't know what will! To preface this review, all of you naysayers out there who shake their heads at sci-fi should remember that, back in the 70's, the names R2-D2, C3PO, Chewie...you get my point, here...were unknowns. Now they are as much a facet of popular literary culture as is Mr. Darcy. Jane Austen, Henry James, Dickens, etc., were beautiful storytellers, but sci-fi has amazingly imaginative beauty surrounding it as well. And this author, Vlane Carter, knows that for a fact....

...there are A LOT of scenes that the reader gets to experience. From the military battle with the UFO, to the alien shark attack on another planet (which is really cool, by the way), this author offers a never-ending parade of amazing creatures and locations that will, perhaps, one day be logged into popular literary culture right beside old C3PO and his little beeping buddy......There are two factions out there in America - Star Wars vs. Star Trek - and I am definitely on the side of George Lucas having the more creative concept. So hats off to this writer, Vlane Carter, who may someday join those Lucas ranks if readers and sci-fi fans everywhere band together and realize that the force really MAY be with this one." – **FEATHERED QUILL REVIEWS.**

"....the bialien trilogy is not your typical sci-fi novel. Think of a comic book that uses words instead of illustrations and you might come close. One thing that the writer certainly has is imagination. It is written very visually....

.....you may tell by his style that Vlane is very passionate about his writing. It takes time and effort to envision and write a novel of this length without losing the energy throughout it. Bialien is his first novel, and, from his marketing material and website, certainly not his last. It is always interesting to see the first story written and how writing styles evolve from book to book. Let's see where Volume Two takes us." –**TOP BOOK REVIEWERS.**

"A Sci-Fi series set on exploring concepts of the deep future, "The Bialien Trilogy" is for the Science fiction fan who likes to be amazed at what the future holds...." - **MIDWEST BOOK REVIEWS**

-"Vlane Carter first novel is a huge "tome" of a book. There is lots of action and adventure as our main character, Jaden, meets a host of aliens from across the universe, engages in a host of battles as well as doing some "fun" stuff. There is a lot of "things" in this book to cause the reader to pause and ponder. For the adventurous reader who likes long novels make sure you put this close to the top of your Must Read list.—**STEVEN FIVECATS, EDITOR. YELLOW30 SCI-FI REVIEW.**

"...the first thing readers will notice about this book is the author's manner of storytelling. It's different and can take some getting use to. That said, if you adjust your thinking to the author's way of telling the story, you'll find that it works! He achieves his goal of making the story read as if you're seeing it on the big screen, as an action packed movie. Also worth mentioning, is that to complete the entire scope of the story, Vlane has placed visual images throughout, as well as a book sound track, creating an entirely new dimension to the meaning of author/story/reader interaction....

....Outside of the book itself, this author takes great care to interact with his readers and has a website that includes free chapter plus loads of information about the series. Inside the book, he takes just as much care, and it's clear he has put his entire being into each and every word. Real knowledge can make or break a book, and this author definitely knows his technology. ....

....Give this book a chance and you won't be disappointed by the in your face, non-stop action that leaves you on a roller coaster ride that thrusts you up and down, side to side, both thrills and chills, and then rockets you out of this world..."

-New Reads Underground. Rachel M. D'aigle, NRU Head and Author of YA Fantasy Series The Journals of The Jacoby Odyssey

....This book crosses many topics, from government conspiracies, alien technology, nanotechnology, world domination, love, female empowerment and religion... All which take the reader into new realms of thought and possibility, allowing for outside the box thinking and discussion amongst readers.....

....Sci-fi and fiction enthusiasts will have a hard time putting this book down. Vlane Carter succeeds in his unconventional storytelling style, drawing readers into his vast creation, while the plot twists keep you riveted and guessing until the books final page. Or, make that the final word...." **-M. Penny Harmon, Review SIP "ReviewSIP" (Salt Lake City, Utah)**

BIAlien - Rise of the BIAliensapien: Human Evolved book 1,2 & 3 (vol I)

BIO-Sapien books 1,2,3,4,5,6 (Vol I)

TO ALL READERS AND BOOK CRITICS PLEASE NOTE:

BIO-Sapien was written in present tense for the following reasons:

1. So the reader can read and experience the novel as if they were watching a movie.
2. Nanotime.
3. Detailed action sequences.
4. Movie soundtracks inserted into different parts of the story.
5. Telepathic communication and talking to another personality.
6. Mind reading and answering questions inside of a conversation.
7. Have the reader experience the story as if they are right with Jaden at all times.

"....Author, Vlane Carter, has created a story told in a unique and unconventional writing style, keeping the action in the present tense, so as to keep the reader feeling as though they are experiencing the action as its happening. It can be akin to reading a script, or make you feel as though you're watching a movie. It is a writing style that can, at first, be jarring and difficult to understand. But if you give it a few chapters it will not only grow on you, but draw you in. And then you suddenly cannot imagine the story written any other way. And, quite possibly, it could be the first book that includes its own music recommendations (to listen to while reading)....." - **M. Penny Harmon, Review SIP "ReviewSIP"**

Single quotes ' ' are used in the book when:

To show main character Jaden communicating with his alien friend AI (located in his mind).
High-speed telepathic communications.

WHAT HAPPENED IN "BIO-Sapien 1 & 2?"

PLOT/SYNOPSIS

The evil Darclonians (formerly known as Robogods) used to be an all robotic species, but have been using organic bodies for the past 150,000 years in search of the perfect host for their experiment. The robotic droids scanned millions of solar systems to find a planet the right distance from the Sun that could support life. Over 100,000 years ago a droid fired small comets filled with sextillions of Nanomoles towards Earth. Reaching the lower atmosphere, the comets had exploded and dispersed Nanomoles which sought out organic and intelligent life. Undetectable, the parasites have since been sitting in their host's brains learning the biology and recording the human experience from generation to generation. They have been awaiting a signal from a mothership which will activate an 84 hour, three stage countdown.

The good Andromedians (from the Andromeda galaxy) needed a purpose for humans as well. They are peaceful explorers and have been in several battles with Darclonians over the years. Their dilemma is their Biomechanical bodies would be destroyed in their ships when they use Optic-warp to exit the Milky-way's center super massive blackhole in subspace. They have been monitoring a lot of Darclonian activity in this galaxy and needed a way to investigate it. They used one of their older class ships with Artificial intelligence on it to seek out an intelligent human being on Earth, to see if the body can make it to their Galaxy in one piece. This is when Jaden Marino finds the UFO.

On a cold winter evening in 2000, Jaden Marino, discovers a UFO near his home in upstate NY. The government detects it and swarms the area on a full-scale UFO hunt. Unable to find the now invisible UFO, the government follows Jaden to it after listening to him excitedly disclose it to a friend on the telephone.

On the run from the persistent government wanting him for "further questioning," he hides inside of the UFO made of liquid metal nanotechnology. Meanwhile, the government tries to take the craft to

<u>Area 51</u>. Inside the ship, Jaden's body goes into a comatose state, and he has an out-of-the-body experience. The spaceship translates his English language and math capabilities from his mind into its alien language, subsequently enabling him to control the UFO with his mind.

Jaden manages to pilot the ship, escaping the government. As he gets used to controlling the ship by pure thought, the government sends all of their best and top-secret aircraft to intercept and destroy the spacecraft. Jaden uses microscopic autonomous alien eyes, called nanoeyes, which allow him to see outside the ship in dozens of directions, as well as smell, taste, and feel. The nanoeyes transform into nanoscanners when they detect a threat. Nanoscanners can scan through any non-shielded aircraft and learn its defenses in seconds.
Jaden quickly learns the capabilities of the UFO and engages the best government pilots in an intense chase over New York. Jaden outruns missiles and can actually see bullets moving past the UFO. The intense chase creates dozens of powerful <u>sonic booms</u>, the impact of which breaks windows and causes citizens' ears to ring. <u>Jaden rescues an SR-71 Blackbird aircraft that flies past its maximum ceiling height. Jaden's quick thinking activates a tractor beam in an attempt to stop the SR-71 Blackbird from crashing into a house.</u>

Jaden races a top-secret <u>Blackbird</u> from New York City to Chicago at Mach 7, just missing an airliner that was about to land. Jaden realizes he is at the maximum speed on Earth and is trying to explore the speed of light engines. He overrides the light engine controls in an attempt to outrun the Blackbird. The engines of the UFO charge to 0.1% the speed of light and Jaden is over North Korea in a split second. Jaden loses control of the ship and it flies on autopilot away from Earth's orbit. The UFO accelerates and takes a quick thirty-minute ride to Jupiter, where it explores the inner layers of this giant planet. Jaden's mind is blown away when he sees Jupiter up close.

<u>The UFO then explores Jupiter's moon Europa and Jaden has his first alien encounter with thousands of species of alien sea life. The glow-in-the-dark animals are intriguing to Jaden at first.</u> Jaden then encounters intelligent, coordinated alien sharks that greet him by

biting different parts of the UFO. Being integrated with the UFO, Jaden's body feels what the ship feels. Eventually the ship tries to leave the moon Europa, but not before being swallowed by a mother shark and taking her to the surface of the moon with the ship.

The UFO sets a course towards the sun. The craft travels through space by using an advanced space traveling method called optic-warp. This system allows the UFO to travel in subspace after being broken into a quadrillion molecules, which allows the ship to pass a light-year every 7-90 seconds.

The UFO eventually sets a course to planet Xenos (Andromedian's home planet), they are captured by a Darclonian colony in the Andromeda Galaxy, 2.1 million light-years from Earth. His body was experimented on and the Darclonians realized there is some value in humans. This sets off a chain of events for Earth and a mothership is dispatched. Jaden and the ship are later rescued by an elite Andromedian biomechanical team lead by BELLONA.

Bellona, Marco and Bomani, who range in age from 50,000-69,000 years old, make their debut appearance. Marco and Bellona show off a few of their superhero skills and advanced weapons as they take on an army of blisters, cubfighters and skelborgs. Bellona fights at super speeds with her anti-hydrogen energy sword while dodging a hail of meteorites hitting the ground around her. Marco also shows his stealth and advanced weaponry skills. These highly skilled, peaceful warriors are shocked when they see a new threat to their galaxy. The dark energy knight makes its first appearance. They hit it with dozens of torpedoes from their ships and then leave to return Jaden to their home planet.

Jaden wakes up discovering he is on another planet called Xenos, and is in a virtual under water city in an artificial body. Bellona informs Jaden of everything that has taken place and Jaden learns about a chain of events that is unfolding for Earth.

While on Xenos, Jaden plays in the Andromedian's futuristic gravity games; flies around the planet without a body by using nanoeyes; observes the planet's gravity tides; wars; joins a space team; races in exoskeleton intergalactic spaceships (EIS) and plays a virtual game of chess with alien pieces.

Bellona befriends Jaden and is his personal escort while he is a guest on Xenos. Bellona unintentionally develops a special interest for Jaden (Bellona used to be a carbon life form in her past life). She tries to understand his Catholic beliefs and explains her people's long history on religion, technology and why he is there.

Even though ten years has passed on Earth, Jaden's human body has only aged a few weeks. He misses his family, friends and girlfriend back on Earth. Jaden's travel to the Andromeda Galaxy sets off a chain of events for Earth. Jaden learns of a Darclonian mother ship leaving from another part of the Milky Way Galaxy and heading towards Earth. There are conflicts in the Andromedian elder council on whether it is too dangerous for Jaden to return to Earth by himself. Jaden later proves himself worthy to one elder.

The Andromedians pack Jaden full of prototype organic nanotechnology called nanodrones. The nanodrones run Jaden's body like crewmembers on the Star Trek Enterprise. The quadrillions of nanodrones modify his brain and DNA for optimum performance.

BIO-Sapien book 3

Book 3 starts off with Jaden returning to Earth in his upgraded EIS, eighteen years later by earth time.

His bio-engineered body is slowly evolving into superhuman levels. His mission is to help scientist locate the Nanomole in humans and then deactivate it, before the Darclonian mothership enters broadcast range. When a Nanomole is activated and is in the correct stage, it can control a human body. It would need to synchronize with a Bio-parasite for a permanent takeover of the human mind (Bio-parasites are Darclonians in microbe form). Love and romance follows the chapters as the silent attack on humans begins.

BIO-Sapien book 3 – Human Metamorphosis

Chapter 12: The Rebirth of a Legend

EARTH, ALBANY, NY STATE TRAUMA HOSPITAL 79°F
WEDNESDAY SEPTEMBER 3, 2018   3:12 AM

Two male emergency medical technicians are standing outside the emergency room on a break. One is smoking a cigarette and the other is drinking coffee. They are having a conversation with each other.

"I tried that *Third Virtual Life* last night at home online, it wasn't the same as being in the virtual fantasy store," EMT 1 says.

"Yeah, I know what you mean, the store has the full body connection to strap into. Two weeks ago, I went to the store on Main Street and I was having sex with a girl that lived in Texas. It totally felt like the real thing. Women are easy online; we had sex on a cloud then in the White House. Then when my time was up, I got out of the virtual dome I had released all over my underwear," EMT 2 says.

"Oh my god, that's the best. I have to get the Internet 2.0 connection in my house. I still have the old Internet...." EMT 1 is interrupted by an eerie sound behind him.

Jaden's unconscious body appears curled up on the stretcher in the fetal position. His body begins to shake uncontrollably as his body goes into shock.

"Shit, where did this guy come from? What is all this slimy shit around him?" EMT 1 asks while he drops his coffee.

"I don't know, but put on your gloves and let's get him inside."

The EMTs roll the stretcher a few feet into the hospital emergency entrance doors. EMT 1 straightens Jaden's body so that he is laying flat on his back. EMT 2 puts an oxygen mask over Jaden's face. Two tubes in the mask go up Jaden's nostrils like little snakes. A thick coolant mist goes into his nasal-cavity and upper throat membranes and evaporates. This procedure is slowly lowering Jaden's brain and body temperature. EMT 1 talks on a small earpiece and pushes buttons on the side of it. Straps automatically come out from the sides of the stretcher to hold Jaden still. The EMTs are both on a side of Jaden and pushing him down a long hallway. A beam of blue light comes from the ceiling and onto Jaden's body. Suddenly a red light comes from under the sheets on the stretcher. The lights disappear simultaneously and two nurses appear. Jaden's left arm is slightly penetrated by the stretcher. A small LCD screen comes up from the top of the stretcher. Nurse 1 gives Jaden an injection into his arm.

"Virtual x-ray 3D complete and MRI-4D is complete. Where did you pick him up from?" Nurse 2 asks.

"He just appeared out of nowhere and was lying on a stretcher," EMT 2 says.

"Yeah okay, were you smoking in your ambulance again?" She asks.

Nurse 1 looks at the screen; the virtual x-ray shows his spinal cord is being crushed, and his blood pressure very high. He also has internal bleeding in a few places. They quickly roll Jaden into an operating room.

"His heart rate is 210. His outside body DNA scan is coming up as an error on the LCD screen. The computer is running his blood DNA now," nurse 2 says.

The EMTs stay outside the room. A robotic body with a ten-inch LCD screen as a face walks into the operating room. The screen has a human face on it. Dr. Hoswer shows in small letters under his face. Over the screen are two cameras moving together like eyes.

"Who is the patient?" Dr. Howser asks from the robot's mouth, while the hands touch different parts around Jaden's body.

Jaden coughs up liquid and blood. The mask automatically sucks up the liquid and blood. Two technicians run to the room to help. He calms down and stops shaking. A few nanodrones get to work around Jaden's organs. They mimic and assist the coolant mist in his nose cavity.

Nurse 1 replies, "We don't know yet. He doesn't have an embedded RFID, criminal microchip, or Medicaid chip," Pam says.

"Get those liquid samples scanned. This male in his early 20's looks like he has symptoms of the bends," the doctor says.

"Bends?" The second nurse, Kiesha, asks.

"Yes, bends, decompression sickness. First level blood scan shows excess nitrogen in his blood and his body looks as if he was deep underwater somewhere. We will have to put him in a decompression unit, after we get more IVs in him," the doctor explains.

"His local and national DNA blood scan isn't showing anything. HIV1-4, hepatitis and other diseases are showing all negative," Nurse Pam says.

"His DNA structure looks very strange as if it was modified. The MRI-4D is showing very little brain activity. Increase his oxygen and get John Doe to the decompression room. Put a back and neck brace under him," Howser says.

A technician put a brace on Jaden and they roll him down the hallway toward an elevator. A nurse follows from behind the stretcher with a portable LCD screen in her hand watching Jaden's vitals.

"How is his blood temperature at 93.2°F already?" Kiesha asks.

"I don't know. It was at 100.4°F, when we first bought him into the hospital ten minutes ago," technician 1 says.

"Obviously you have mistaken, he must have been suffering from hypothermia when he got here," Kiesha says with an attitude.

There is silence and the men have confused looks on their faces. She presses a button on the oxygen mask and the tubes come out of his nose. The technicians talk to each other in low voices.

"This is our first John Doe in two years," technician 1 says.

"Yeah, this guy looks wasted," technician 2 says.

"Yeah, look at his clothes and the old NY Giants jersey. His jersey probably would have been worth something on Zbay if he didn't take a swim in a swamp," technician 2 says while laughing.

Technician 1 laughs, "He fell asleep in the 90's and woke up in the teens."

They move Jaden to a small decompression room and they lock the door. He is still unconscious with IVs and body monitors all over his body. He is lying in a small decompression room by himself.

Inside of his body, the rest of the nanodrones go online. They come out of his cells and tissues. They go inside of his brain and begin reconstructing his memory. The nanodrones begin to repair things around his body. Ninety minutes goes by and they bring him up to a room on the seventh floor.

"Well you won't need this, Mr. John Doe," Nurse Pam says, while she helps a technician move the back brace.

The sun begins to rise. The sunlight shines through the windows and onto Jaden's body. The fresh summer breeze comes through the window from under a television and hits his body. The cool air moves through his clothes and awakens the hairs around his body. His nose interprets the natural smelling air from the trees. He opens his eyes for the first time and looks around. Everything is blurry as he tries to focus on objects. He blinks his eyes a few times trying to adjust to the bright light over him. He sees a middle-aged chubby white woman in a nurse uniform looking at him smiling. Jaden notices he is in a patient's gown.

"Hello there, you're awake; did you have a nice rest?" She asks.

Jaden looks confused and doesn't respond.

"What is your name sir?"

"How are you feeling?" She asks.

He doesn't respond because the speech and auditory cortex parts of his brain are still offline. He just sees her moving her mouth. More nanodrones enter Jaden's brain. He feels strange tingling sensations around his body.

"Well just press this button, if you need me," she says while walking away.

A robotic body with an LCD screen as a face comes into Jaden's room. He turns to look at it with a nervous expression on his face. Suddenly his hearing comes back, but it comes back very loud with a ringing sound. He sits up holding his ears as the volume goes down and ringing disappears. He hears echoes of voices.

"Hey buddy, are you okay? What's wrong?" The robotic human screen face asks.

Nurse Pam walks back into the room.

"He can't speak yet," she says.

"I can speak now," Jaden says.

"Well excuse me," she says while walking to the other side of the bed, checking the bedside LCD screen for his vitals.

"Hello, John Doe, I'm Dr. Mayflower. Your vitals look much better. I think the MRI-4D scan made a mistake a few hours ago when it showed problems with your body. The new scan shows your bones, body structure and internal organs look fine now. I'm surprised to see your eyes open now; you were presumed brain dead. Were you night scuba diving somewhere in a lake or ocean?"

"I don't know," Jaden replies.

"What is your name? Where do you live?" Mayflower asks.

"I don't know," he says.

"Do you remember anything?"

There is silence as Jaden thinks, holding his hand to his chin. So much information is being shuffled around his mind.

"I think I just traveled from a nearby galaxy and I'm supposed to be warning the government on a future alien attack," Jaden says.

There is an awkward silence as they both stare at him in disbelief.

"Is there anything else you remember?" The doctor asks.

"Not now, but I would like to know why are you talking through a robot body and your face is on the screen?" Jaden asks.

"Doctors at night aren't required to be in the hospital. They can remote in through these R.H.I.U. or robotic human interface unit. I'm currently in Los Angeles and I'm covering a night shift for another doctor. I see everything through the two camera eyes, above the screen. My body here is fully connected into the robot unit. Where have you been, Mr. John Doe? These have been around for a few years now."

"I'm trying to figure that out," Jaden says.

Jaden can't believe how advanced technology has gotten on Earth.

"Well relax and get some rest. Some people will be by later to ask you some questions," the doctor says while walking away in an all white robot body. The odd clanking sounds of the feet walking echo around the room.

"Doctor!" Jaden yells as he stops walking and continues, "What day is today?"

He turns around and says, "Wednesday September 3, 2018."

The robot continues to walk away, while taking irregular sounding footsteps.

"Well, I'll turn on the TV for you to watch," Nurse Pam says.

Suddenly the wall lights up as a television appears over the window. He hears the sounds from the television from different directions. He turns his head and looks all around the room.

"That is 12.1 Dolby stereo sound you hear all around you," the nurse says.

She walks out of the room and talks to the doctor in the hallway. Jaden turns his head towards them standing by a nursing station. He zooms in on them and is able to hear what they are saying.

"Nurse, make sure you keep monitoring this John Doe, a lot of things aren't making any sense. This guy just came out of nowhere, he has no records, no DNA on file anywhere and we can't get any DNA samples from him," Mayflower says.

"No DNA on him? I gave you a sample of his hair and skin earlier," Pam says.

"I know you did, the lab keeps saying it is an invalid sample and the DNA/RNA structure is missing. I've never seen this before, his blood is coming back abnormal. This person might also be mentally unstable. Get the psychologist that comes in at seven to interview him ASAP. I'm taking a break; this electronic body suit is giving me a headache. Send me a brain text if anything develops. Thank you nurse."

"Okay doctor, I'll get on it."

They walk away from each other and the robotic body goes into a room with other robotic bodies. It stands on a designated area and it is powered down. Jaden is confused to how he was able to hear the conversation from so far away. The TV on the wall grabs his attention.

"Good morning America. I'm Jake and this is Michelle and we are live on BNN this morning," the male on the television says.

'BNN sounds so familiar,' Jaden says to himself, while the T.V continues.

"It was just eight months ago this week that Vice President Stefanie Paylin took the commander-in-chief position and was sworn in. The inexperienced Alaskan governor was the running mate with President J. Macarthur. Macarthur had a sudden heart attack early this year and died at the age of 76. She has become the 46th President and the first female President. She nominated the Secretary of Defense Kevin Robinson earlier to vice president. Robinson, also in his seventies, has served the military all his life and received the Purple Heart for his heroism in the Gulf War in the early nineties. He has since been with the Pentagon in top-secret government projects; including being a major player of

N.G.D. (Next Generation of Defense). Robinson has been known as someone for getting the job done for his country...." Michelle reports.

Robinson's much older face is shown in a close up on the TV while he is at the White House at a birthday party for one of Paylin's children.

"Shit, I remember now. That asshole was trying to kill me. It is all coming back to me now," he says while he continues to watch the television.

Michelle continues, "...A spokesman for the Pentagon says N.G.D. involves a highly classified prototype quantum diamond processing supercomputer called Motherdrone..."

Jaden falls asleep thinking about who he is.

'Who am I? Who am I?' He asks himself.

Two hours pass and his body is fully healed. A technician walks into his room to take MRI-4D scans and virtual x-rays from his bed. He leaves the room.

A commercial comes on the television. A middle-aged man stands there with his body completely covered in a thin, black body suit. His eyes are covered in all black goggles. He is moving his arms around.

"...Strap into Nextbox 3 the next generation of virtual reality gaming. Create your own worlds of video games. Play paintball from home, swim underwater in your swimming pool at real Bahamas' underwater locations, and take classes across the country... Adult world is now online. Why date real women, when you can have a virtual date? Strap into a new world of virtual reality. Internet 2.0 required, not suggested for pregnant women, and people who experience seizures."

The news comes back on Michelle and Jake is talking.

"...Electric bills around the country have been greatly decreasing thanks to the technology of enhanced geothermal energy drilling. This new process has proved successful over the past three years in providing fifteen percent of the electricity for the USA. The process involves injecting high-pressure water three to four miles deep into the crust and rocks. The heated water returns to the surface in steam and turns turbines to create electricity for homes," Michelle says.

"That is amazing Michelle, every day we are being less dependent on gas. I heard that next generation wind turbines on our coast lines are producing another fifteen percent of electricity for our country," Jake says.

"Looks like the green technologies are in a neck and neck race," she says as they both chuckle.

"In other news, the national debt has reached a record 19.5 trillion dollars last month and with a public portion of 14.3 trillion dollars. This is due to years of hyperinflation, Iraq War and new healthcare spending that started in 2010. The countries we are borrowing from, including China, increased their interest over the years on the money we owe them. China has become the new super power of the world over the years. President Paylin has vowed to reduce the United States defense budget by seventy-five percent to help balance the federal budget. Something republicans are one hundred percent against. She also suggested congress passes a bill to use fifteen percent of our gold reserves to pay off some of the national debt. House speaker Perry says the President has very little support for the bill in congress…The democrats and republicans agreed the debt should be paid by future generations," Jake says.

Jaden wakes up and feels the sun shining brightly over him. He pulls the plugs and monitors from his body. The nurse rushes into the room.

"Sir, you cannot take those off, please sit on your bed," Pam says.

"I'm feeling better. I have to inform the President of an attack on Earth," Jaden says while lying back down.

"Tell me more about these attacks on Earth and who you are, Mr. John Doe," a man with a dark blue suit and baldhead walks into the room saying.

Jaden turns to him, "I know this sounds a little crazy, but I was on another planet called Xenos in the Andromeda Galaxy. I left Earth in 2000 and now I'm back. It's a lot to explain, but these bad aliens called Darclonians are on their way to Earth. The Darclonians infected us humans many years ago with these nanomoles that record our memories and can temporarily control us. So this is why I have to inform the government and President about what is about to take place."

"How did you travel to this Andromeda Galaxy? Did you use a Stargate?" The man in the suit asks.

"Wait a second, who are you, anyway?" Jaden asks.

24

"I'm Dr. Brown, the hospital psychologist."

"Why am I wasting my time talking to you? I thought you were a detective or something. I have to go," Jaden says while getting out of the bed.

"Mr. John Doe, I would suggest you get back into the bed and finish answering my questions," Dr. Brown says.

"You can take your questions and shove it up your tight ass. I'm not explaining myself to you. I'm out of here. Where are my clothes?" Jaden asks.

"Sorry your clothes are being analyzed for DNA samples, since we can't identify who you are from your body DNA," Dr. Brown says in a firm voice.

Jaden walks towards the window and looks out into the parking lot. He notices he is on the third floor of the building. There are dozens of trees across the street and he can see the wind shaking the branches.

"Mr. Doe, please sit back on the bed so that no one gets hurt here," Pam pleads.

Suddenly two men with blue bionic exoskeleton suits walk into the room. They have security guard badges on the outside of their hard plastic body suits. The bionic suit has many small yellow wires outside the suit going down the arms and legs. The wires run straight into a special helmet around the head. The men have clear goggles around their eyes showing information like a computer screen. Special microchip embedded gloves are covering their hands.

"Mr. John Doe, please get back into your bed or we will use force on you," security guard 1 says.

"Force on me? I'm not afraid of you fake Robocop freaks," Jaden says.

He walks up to the guards blocking the door. He gets into his karate stance and throws a straight punch into guard 2's chest. The striking blow doesn't faze the guard.

"That's all you got you little punk. Punch harder, maybe you'll break the bones in your hand," guard 2 says.

"Stop this, immediately," Dr. Brown says while standing back.

Jaden concentrates on his right arm and his muscles tighten. Small bubbles form inside his skin and run up and down his right arm. The nanodrones in his muscle tissue in the lower back, waist and upper thighs are being strengthened. Nanodrones protect and strengthen the bones in his fist.

"I have some more for you!" Jaden yells.

He swings again and hits the guard with a more powerful blow in his chest. The punch makes a dent in the hard plastic armor. The guard loses his balance and falls backwards onto the nursing station knocking over a small computer screen. The air is knocked out of him. The other guard looks in disbelief.

"Wow that was amazing. I never hit anyone that hard before. Oh no, I feel so weak now," Jaden says in a moaning voice.

The other guard grabs Jaden around his arms and body from behind. He can't move, but he kicks his feet wildly. The guard slams him on the bed. The nurse injects Jaden with something to calm him down. The guard puts handcuffs around his wrist and cuffs him to the bed. Jaden closes his eyes and opens them. The room is moving around very slowly and he passes out. The nurse checks on the security guard that fell down. She comes back into the room.

"Notify the sheriff that we have a B1 John Doe patient going to Central Mental Ward," Brown says while reviewing his charts and x-rays.

"Yes, doctor," the nurse says.

"Also, check him for more drugs and diseases," the doctor says.

"Yes, doctor."

"Okay doctor, if you need us we will be down the hall," guard 1 says while he helps partner down the hall.

"I lost my balance when he hit me, man," guard 2 pleads while walking down the hall holding his chest while breathing heavily.

A few nurses, doctors and more security guards are in the hallway trying to see what is going on. Some transport workers come into the room. They uncuff him and lift him onto a transport stretcher then re-cuff him. The transporter pushes him into the hallway while all the nurses and hospital workers look at him. Two female nurses begin to talk to each other.

"That cute guy said he is from another planet?" Nurse 3 asks nurse 4 while they both look at him being rolled towards the elevator.

"Yeah girl, I wonder if he is single," nurse 4 says.

"Are you crazy?"

26

"At least he just got checked out for every disease. Lord knows there is a shortage of men these days that are disease free. I can deal with a man with some mental issues. He also maybe never played *Third Virtual Life* or *Adult World*," nurse 4 says.

"Hmmm... My husband stopped touching me after playing that sick game," nurse 3 says.

"I had to pay for a guy on a date last month because he has a rent to own R.F.E.C. at home and doesn't have the money to date a female."

"Shit, you mean to tell me he had the money to buy a robotic female entertainment companion?" Nurse 3 says.

"Yeah, he said he doesn't date women and doesn't want to get married."

"That is sick, I would kill my husband if he bought one of those nasty sex robots home. My husband doesn't even want to have any more kids with me because he is on birth control and..." Nurse 3 says.

The elevator door opens, and Jaden is still unconscious. They roll him through a side exit. His body shakes for a second then stops. Something enters into his brain and changes in size.

"Did you see that?" Escort 1 asks.

"I did, but I wish I didn't. I'm just trying to get this weirdo in the sheriff's van. I'm getting bad vibes from him," escort 2 says.

"Where is the van? These guys are late."

Jaden still unconscious hears voices.

'Jaden, wake up. What is going on? Where are you being transported too?' AI asks telepathically.

"Jaden? AI is that you? I'm Jaden, that's right," Jaden mumbles in a confused tone.

'Jaden, you're talking out loud and other people can hear you. Think telepathically like you were doing before. Also don't say your name out loud,' AI orders.

"Other people? Where are you hiding at AI? Are you still in the Gravhawk?" Jaden asks in a delirious voice.

There is silence while the escorts look at Jaden as if he is crazy.

"The van just pulled up, let's go," escort 2 says.

They quickly push him towards the van.

"Hey fellas how is it going today?" Officer Randy asks with a country accent.

The middle-aged officer with red hair and beard with sunglasses on looks over the paper work.

"It's going fine. This one is talking to himself," escort 1 says.

"We got a John Doe here huh? I haven't seen one of these in years. No identification whatsoever?"

"Nothing at all. We don't know where he came from," escort 2 says.

"Let's get this bad puppy all properly wrapped up for his new home," Randy says.

Jaden opens his eyes and looks around. He sees his hands cuffed to a chain that leads down to his stomach and feet.

'Jaden, it's me again AI.'

Jaden tries to talk, but can't.

'Talk telepathically, remember?' AI asks.

'Okay, I remember, what did you do to me? My voice is gone,' Jaden says telepathically.

'I temporarily disabled your voice. You were talking aloud to these humans. That isn't the best idea right now. I also removed that drug they put into your bloodstream, this is why you suddenly woke up.'

'Where have you been all this time?' He asks.

'I was parking the ship in a safe spot and I had to make sure our ship wasn't detected by humans and the Darclonians mother ship long range radar. That required a few hours. Why are you in handcuffs and being transported by an armed man?' AI asks.

'They think I'm crazy, because I told them about me being on another planet and warning the government about the Darclonians being on their way here,' Jaden explains.

'That could only mean...'

'Psychiatric ward hospital,' they say at the same time.

'This is a weird future...' Jaden says while being interrupted.

'I leave you alone for a few hours and you get yourself on your way to a mental hospital.'

'I wasn't thinking right; I didn't even know my name or who I was for awhile. I'm remembering things little by little,' Jaden explains.

'I understand, listen, when your body was reassembled from optic-warp something in your brain was disrupting your brain functions. Your neurons in your brain were going crazy and then it stopped when we got to Earth. Your mind needed time to

28

reorganize itself more than what was estimated before. Therefore, I dropped you off at the trauma hospital and flew very low to the North Pole. The nanodrones went online ASAP to help get your body in normal condition,' AI says.

'Where are you now then?'

'I'm in your brain. I entered through the back of your spinal cord. Your nervous system jumped. Then I had to ride your bloodstream into your brain. I'm in a part of your brain where another personality would be at. You have mazes and mazes of neurons in your brain.'

'That is good to know. How can I break out of these chains and get out of this situation,' Jaden asks while moving his chains around making clinging sounds.

"Hey buddy, relax you have a twenty minute drive ahead of you. You are not going anywhere in those chains. I'm taking you to your new home," Officer Randy says.

'There isn't much you can do now. I have to calculate what weapons your human body will be capable of. This could take hours, days or weeks,' AI says.

'Are you crazy? That long? I can't survive in a mental ward that long. I want to see my girlfriend and family. I also have to warn the government on where to look in space to get the communications sent to stop the Darclonians mind nanomole attack,' Jaden says in a nervous voice.

"..."

'Turn my voice back on,' Jaden demands.

Jaden clears his throat.

"How are you officer? How long will I be at the psychiatric hospital?" Jaden asks while looking up towards the white ceiling of the van.

"You are a B1 patient, you'll be there two to four weeks minimum," the officer says while looking into the rear view mirror at Jaden lying on his back.

"Shit!" Jaden yells.

"I can talk to the doctors there and I can talk them down to having you there for one to two weeks minimum. Only, if you can tell me your name and how you got to the hospital. You'll enter as a C1 patient, less security and you'll be able to do more in there," Officer Randy says.

'Jaden, don't tell him your name. You could have warrants on your name and you don't need the wrong government catching you without a way to defend yourself,' AI says.

'Warrants? From eighteen years ago? I don't think anyone is looking for me now,' Jaden says.

'Just give him a fake name, trust me. I think the government has better things to worry about than a teenager who disappeared eighteen years ago,' AI says.

"I'm Henry Cooper, and I'm twenty years old," Jaden yells.

"What town are you from? Do you know your social security number?" Randy asks.

'Shit, this asshole is asking me too many questions,' Jaden says to AI and himself.

"I'm from Troy, New York. I don't remember my social security number."

"Thanks for remembering for me. We will be there in ten minutes. I'll see what I can do for you," Randy says while touching the front windshield looking up some information.

Jaden's body shakes as the van goes over potholes. The chain clinging gives him an eerie feeling around his body.

'Are the nanoscanners or eyes working yet?' Jaden asks.

'No, they are being configured now and are offline,' AI says.

'I wanted to see what was going on outside and which highway we are on,' Jaden says.

'Doesn't matter now, we are here,' AI says.

They pull into a gated area outside the huge complex. There are two guards with bionic upper body suits at the gate verifying Randy's paperwork. The officer drives his van to the patient entrance. He stops and is met by two workers in all white uniforms.

"Here is another one for you," Randy says as he gets out the van and walks around back.

"There have been a lot of mental patients coming in the last few months. We are getting full here. I have never seen so many patients coming in here with unexplainable mental issues. We have scientists, biologists, neuroscientists and a retired psychologist from around the country here," Williams the patient transporter says.

Williams, a black man in his late twenties with a beard and soft brown eyes, smiles at the officer. They roll Jaden and the stretcher out of the van and onto the ground. The sunlight feels good on Jaden's body. Officer Randy approaches Jaden and looks him directly into eyes.

"You're a liar, Mr. Cooper. All seven Henry Coopers in New York have RFIDs and two have criminal microchips. You don't have any. There are no Henrys on file in the entire United States with your DNA blood information. People know better than to lie to law enforcement these days. Now you have one star against you going in here," Randy says with an angry face.

Jaden just looks at him, while he is pushed away still in his hospital gown. The officer stands there smoking a cigar keeping his eyes on him.

"Hey wait a second!" Randy yells.

They stop pushing and Randy walks over with a bag in his hand.

"Here are the rest of his belongings," he says while handing it to Mike the other patient transporter.

'How did he know I was lying so fast?' Jaden asks.

'Technology has changed greatly since you were last on Earth. Governments have better ways of tracking people these days,' AI says.

"Hey buddy, what did you do to piss off Sheriff Randy?" Williams asks Jaden.

"I just gave him a fake name."

"Yeah, buddy I don't know where you been, but people don't do that anymore. The most I've seen people do was having fake RFIDs or scrambled embedded microchips. I think you better tell them something real, before they hook you up to the DSN machine."

"DSN machine?" Jaden asks.

"Yes, it is an experimental machine that scans your mind and tells them everything they need to know. It is a second-generation machine from the lie detector 2.0. They have been trying it on mental patients at will, not even knowing the long-term effects on the brain. What is your nationality, Mr. Cooper?" Williams asks while pulling the stretcher from the front.

"I'm bi-racial; I'm half black and half white," Jaden says.

31

"Cool, just like our former black President. Sir, can you walk?" Williams asks. "We have to give the stretcher back to the sheriff."

"Yes, I can walk. Black President? Meaning, as in President of the United States?" Jaden asks in a confused voice.

"Yes, as in the 44th President of the United States in 2012," Williams says while he and Mike lift Jaden up and onto his feet. The long white hospital gown reaches his feet as he slowly walks into the entrance with a confused look on his face.

"Where you been buddy? Everyone knows that, even people locked away years in prison."

'That's unbelievable. I feel like I'm just coming out of prison from another planet. I must have missed so much over the past eighteen years. I wonder if my parents are okay and where my friends are,' Jaden says to AI.

'If I can get on the Internet somehow, I can look up your family and friends. I could also look up information to help prepare your body for its full potential,' AI says.

He walks inside the building and down a long hallway. A doctor walks up with a big syringe with buttons and red lights on it. The transport workers hold Jaden still as he gets nervous of the big needle.

"What the hell is that?" Jaden asks while struggling.

"This is an RFID needle. We are just inserting a chip into your left wrist. This won't hurt much," Doctor Cochman says while giggling.

The doctor inserts the chip into Jaden's arm while he yells.

"Awwww!"

The small microscopic chip goes under his skin and he doesn't bleed.

"That's strange usually there is some blood," Cochman says while he has a Band-Aid in his hand.

The doctor pulls out a glowing wand and goes over Jaden's face a few times with it.

"What was that?"

"Now your face is in the national face recognition database," Williams replies.

"That doesn't sound good," Jaden says.

"The worst is over buddy, now just a blood test and urine," Williams says.

The doctor takes blood from Jaden's right arm. He hands him a cup to go into the room on the right. Jaden walks into the small room with a cup.

'I should shit in this cup and give it back to them,' Jaden says to AI.

'Jaden, you don't want to cause more problems here and get put into a high security area. I need to do many calculations to figure out what powers you will have. Sunlight and being able to surf the web are very important.'

'Okay, Okay, I'll cooperate. You better get working on those calculations fast. I can't take being in this place for too long. I never even heard of this mental hospital before,' he tells AI.

Jaden pees in the small metal cup with sensors inside. He walks back out still in chains. A nurse takes it and walks away. The escorts remove the chains down to his feet and just leave regular handcuffs around his wrists. They continue to walk through a gated area that requires them to be buzzed into. They reach an elevator on the other side. Jaden walks by a few small rooms with people inside of them. Some are in straitjackets talking to themselves. Two are in straitjackets looking out the window and towards the sky like zombies.

"You aren't taking my brain. You aren't taking my mind! Get out of my mind!" A mental patient in a room yells.

"Come on guys, do you have to put me with the real crazy people?" Jaden asks.

"We are just following orders. You already have a strike against you. Two more and you are on the higher floors in maximum security. Twenty-three hours lock down a day and you'll be strapped down to a bed," Williams says.

They get to his room and open the door. They uncuff him and hand him a small bag.

"You can put on these hospital clothes in the bag and a few of your belongings are in there. Have a good day sir," Williams says while he closes the black steel door with silver bars in the middle.

"Yeah, the doctor will be with you soon," Mike says.

"Thank you, Mr. Two Cents Mike," Jaden says sarcastically.

A tray of food and water is left at the door's window.

Jaden puts his bag on the small single cot. The walls are all white, with a three foot by three-foot window with Plexiglas in the rear of the small room. There is a small toilet in the corner of the room. He reaches and takes the water from the tray and drinks it.

'That toilet looks disgusting. I would hate to use that.'

'If you don't eat any food, you won't have to use it. I can control your eating using advanced photosynthesis same as we did on Xenos.'

'Okay, I don't feel hungry. But this room is jail alright,' he says to himself while he walks over to the window and looks out.

The sun shines from behind a cloud into the room, brightly lighting it up.

'The sun feels good. Makes my body tingle. What time is it AI?'

'From calculating the position of where the sun is and the time we left the hospital to now, it's about 10:25 AM,' AI says.

'Speaking of calculating, give me an update,' he says while he looks in the bag.

'So far, we have successfully reprogrammed your white and red blood cells to accept all the nanodrones. Your T-cells have been reprogrammed and replaced. You will never catch a cold or get sick again. Your DNA and RNA genetic code has been modified again. I have a trillion drones in your mind verifying your neural code. Your ears, nose, eyes and taste will be greatly enhanced by tomorrow. Tomorrow you'll be able to hold your breath for thirty minutes or more. Filtered oxygen will be able to be absorbed from your pores to directly into your bloodstream, filtering out nitrogen. Your brain is at thirty percent usage now, when it gets to seventy-five percent you'll be able to multi-task and control multiple things at one time, as simple as walking and talking,' AI says.

'What about my weapon systems?'

'That's going to take more time Jaden. How long, I'm not sure. My processing speed is only one quadrillion calculations per 100 milliseconds. If you took the nanosincoid from Bellona we could both calculate at one quintillion calculations per fifty milliseconds,' AI says.

'I don't know what all these trillion, billion, quadrillion and quintillion milliseconds mean. Tell me in simple meanings what the benefits would have been,' Jaden says.

'Instead of days or weeks to calculate your weapon systems, it would take two days max, with the proper information being downloaded,' AI says.

'Thank you AI Einstein.'

'We need to look up many subjects on the Internet: advanced physics, advanced calculus, nuclear fusion, advance nanotechnology, Earth biology, Astrophysics, rocket science and definitions that weren't translated from your language from when you were on Earth eighteen years ago. Meaning us Andromedian need to convert our definitions with your human advanced science technology definitions. We were only able to convert what you knew eighteen years ago into our translation. We also need the Internet to figure out which natural resources on your planet we can use to create a weapon system to work with your biological body.'

'I gotcha now; I understand,' Jaden says, 'Just make sure I don't turn into an alien or make my outside look different. Last thing I need is to look like a freak.'

Jaden thinks about the freaks in other movies: *Predator*, *Alf*, aliens in *Star Trek* and the *V* lizard aliens.

'Yes sir.'

There is a knock on the door. A security guard opens the door and a doctor walks in. Jaden turns around.

"Hello, Mr. John Doe, I'm Dr. Cochman," he walks in holding an LCD screen that looks like a notepad. He stands over Jaden.

An overweight, white guard around 5'10" 250 lbs stands by the door with an all black material looking similar to a black dry suit just covering his upper body. He looks directly at Jaden by the window. He has a full beard and is missing a front tooth in his mouth. He is bald and has freckles on his face. His lower body looks like work pants. Wires and cables go around the arms to a pair of gloves with small microchips over them. There aren't any cables or wires going to the legs. The door closes and the doctor sits on the end of the bed.

"Sir, please sit down," the doctor politely asks.

Jaden sits down near the pillow of the bed.

"Why is that guard looking at me as if he is a pit bull and I stole his bone?" Jaden asks.

35

"That is Mr. Ruffo; he is the main guard on this floor. He doesn't take any shit from anyone. But don't worry about him, me and you are going to talk," Cochman says in a nice voice.

"They tell me at the hospital you didn't remember your name and you gave the sheriff a fake name. The doctors and nurses at the hospital also tell me you came from another planet. That you have to warn people on Earth of an attack," Cochman says.

"I don't remember saying that. I was confused and couldn't remember much," Jaden says.

The doctor looks at his LCD notebook and words begin to fill in on the screen.

"How are those words going on that screen?" Jaden asks.

"The signal from my mind is going directly onto the notebook screen. It is a lot easier than typing or writing by hand. So you never said in the hospital room, that the vice president of the United States tried to kill you and it is all coming back to you now."

"How did you know I said that, no one was in the room?" Jaden asks.

"We have recording devices all over the place. Are you going to answer the question?"

"I was delusional, I don't know what I was saying," Jaden says.

"You aren't on any drugs, but you did do something to your body. Your fingerprints don't match anything. For some reason we can't get any DNA from your hair, skin or saliva. Do you know why that is?"

Words continue to fill the LCD notebook.

"No, I don't know why it is. Maybe something is wrong with your machine that scans for DNA," Jaden replies.

"Our computer machines have ninety-five percent of every citizen's DNA on file. Your body's DNA shows up as corrupted and our computers have never failed. There is no way you don't have any family in this country. We would be able to locate your family, friends and siblings with the smallest fragment of your DNA. However, nothing is showing up, not even in your blood. Your blood is even showing up some unusual anomalies."

"I don't know why this is Dr. Cockman. Oops I'm sorry, Dr. Cochman," Jaden says while chuckling.

Mr. Ruffo walks over to Jaden with a serious and angry look on his face. Jaden stands up as he quickly approaches. The guard lifts Jaden into the air by his hospital issued white button-up shirt with his left hand and slams him against the wall. Jaden is lifted six inches from the floor. Ruffo's right hand is covered in a glove and is pressed strongly around Jaden's throat, cutting off circulation. Jaden's first reaction was to grab his hand and pull it from his throat to breathe, but he doesn't. He folds his arms instead and looks Ruffo in the eyes with a smirk. Jaden's body absorbs oxygen from his pores around his body. The nanodrones in his blood in his neck push the blood through the tightly compressed veins, towards his brain.

"Listen you little shit, you going to answer what the doctor is asking you. This isn't a game and no time to be making jokes. You are in my house now and you are going to respect Dr. Cochman!" Ruffo yells

"Okay, I'll respect Dr. Cockman," Jaden says with a smile on his face.

Ruffo increases his grip around Jaden's neck, "His name is Cochman."

Jaden has a smile on his face. Thousands of nanodrones race into his throat area strengthening the bone structure, veins and increasing blood flow. The guard releases the grip around his left hand from his shirt and tightens his grip around Jaden's neck.

"Let him go, Ruffo," Cochman calmly says.

"This little shit thinks he can hold his breath."

'Jaden, what is going on? Why is this guy choking you and making your heart rate go up?' AI asks.

'Don't worry about me, just keep calculating and preparing my body. I'm getting to know my new friend here. I can feel the oxygen going into my pores around my body and I feel the carbon dioxide leaving. It feels like a slight breeze on the hairs around my body. My body feels like it's releasing micro farts,' Jaden tells AI.

"Look at me Dr. Cochman, I'm levitating in the air like a genie," Jaden says.

"I don't have time for this," Cochman says.

Ruffo is still staring Jaden in the eyes. Ruffo brings Jaden over to the bed by his neck and head butts him, before dropping him. His body bounces once and a thumping sound is heard. Ruffo walks back towards the corner of the room.

"That's all you got big boy?" Jaden asks, while he touches the small gash on his head. "I'm surprised that bionic suit fits you, I'm sure it was originally made for a cow," he snaps.

Jaden begins breathing again through his lungs. Blood begins to slowly come from his head.

"Listen Mr. John Doe, I see you're not cooperating with us. Maybe you'll cooperate tomorrow," Cochman says while he gets up and walks towards the door.

They leave and Ruffo slams the door and looks at Jaden from the bars.

"We will see you soon and we will get the answers we are looking for you little shit."

"Make sure you find the answers to why you don't have futuristic breath mints in your mouth when you talk to people. Your breath smells like a homeless man's socks," Jaden snaps.

Ruffo walks away with a grin on his face.

'Jaden you are pissing this guy off. We don't need extra problems. My calculations tell me this guy is going to be a problem for us,' AI says.

'I know what I'm doing. I don't like being pushed around by a security guard with a small dick and has something to prove to the world.'

'Okay, you should get some rest. Move the bed closer to the window so we can feel the rays of the sunlight,' AI says.

'I stopped bleeding, cool. That really hurt when he headbutted me.'

Jaden bends down to try to move the bed, but it is bolted to the floor. His arm muscles tighten up and he pulls it harder. It comes off the floor and he moves it towards the window. Jaden looks into the rest of the bag, and sees his wallet. He opens it and everything is missing except fifty-six dollars and a condom.

'Where is my driver's license and credit card?'

'They are in the Gravhawk. I removed them before I dropped you off,' AI says.

'What am I going to do with this outdated condom?'

'I have no idea.'

'Great, maybe I'll try it on to jerk off and I'll have safe sex with myself. Oh man, that was a horrible thought. I'm beginning to think like these people in here,' Jaden says to himself while lying down on the bed.

'You are going to sleep for about twelve hours then I'll wake you up,' AI says.

'Okay. Man, I need a female, it has been years, I mean weeks. I have to try to contact Amy,' he says while he closes his eyes.

Jaden instantly goes into deep delta sleep. Hours go by and he wakes up. It is dark outside and the stars are shining brightly above. Everything is blurry for Jaden as he focuses his eyes. He hears moaning from patients in other rooms. Jaden feels pain in all of his muscles all over his body.

'Why are all my muscles sore and my body in such pain?'

'I turned off a protein in your muscle stem cells. I would need to search the Internet to see if there is an exact word. You will be a lot stronger. I ran hundreds of test on different cells throughout your body, while you were asleep,' AI says.

'Can you do something for the pain?' Jaden asks while sits on his knees and look out the window.

'Thanks, that's better. What time is it about? Why do I feel dizzy?'

'It's about 11 PM. We should get some more sleep. But, first walk around the room,' AI says.

Jaden walks around the room and he does not feel dizzy.

'Stand on the bar at the end of the bed with one foot,' AI says.

'One foot? Okay.'

He jumps up on the bed and stands on one foot on an inch round iron bar.

'The equilibrium in your ears that control your balance has been greatly enhanced. You will also soon be able to walk on walls and ceilings just like in the gravity games.'

'Good work AI, but I'm feeling tired again.'

'Get some more rest I'll wake you up in another ten hours.'

'For some reason I remember the combination lock from when I was in the second grade. I also remember things from when I was one and two years old,' Jaden says while he lies down.

'That is the info from the Darclonian nanomole that was in your brain from when you first left Earth. We decrypted it on our planet and I'm synchronizing many details of your past with your brain. You are going to remember many details of your past. This increase of information is also going to make things in your subconscious come out and give you very realistic dreams. Many areas in your mind are going to be greatly enhanced. You could go

39

back into any day in your past and relive the entire day…' AI says and then stops.

Jaden quickly falls asleep. About three hours go by. He begins to dream.

It is dark, completely dark as he finds himself walking to nowhere. He can't see his hands or body. Not sure what direction he is going or where he is going to. A low voice is heard in the background, the voice gets louder.

"Join us. Join us," the unknown voice says from different areas in the dark.

"Join who? Where is this?"

"We are your destiny…"

"Listen you coward, why don't you turn the lights on and stop hiding in the dark!" Jaden yells.

There is silence and Jaden continues to yell, "Join what? Join your gay orgy? Mafia? Cult? Join a gang? Come out of the closet…"

It suddenly gets very bright. Jaden opens his eyes. It is still dark outside. There are flashlights shining in his face as he tries to cover his eyes. People are walking into his small room. The lights overhead comes on. Two people grab him and hold him down. One of the people is Ruffo in his bionic body suit.

'Jaden what is going on?' AI asks.

'I don't know. Give me some super strength to fight them off,' Jaden says.

'I can't right now. Fighting them isn't going to help the situation. Just go along with whatever they want for now, it's best,' AI says to Jaden.

'Easy for you to say, you are tucked away safely in my brain somewhere.'

A nurse walks over with a needle. Jaden kicks the other guard against the wall.

"Oh, we have a fighter here?" Ruffo asks while leaning directly over Jaden holding him down. His massive strength makes it hard for Jaden to move.

"What are you people doing to me?" Jaden asks them.

"You'll see, I told you we would be back to get those answers," Ruffo says with a smile on his face.

The nurse injects Jaden with the needle into his arm. Ruffo is handed a straitjacket from the other guard. Jaden calms down and they try to put the straitjacket over him.

'What was that I was just injected with?' Jaden asks AI.

'Something to calm you down, I'm going to counter balance the injection. It's already in your brain and bloodstream,' AI says.

They finish wrapping Jaden in the straitjacket. His legs are tied together. The nurse rolls a stretcher into the room. Ruffo single handedly lifts him onto the stretcher and they roll him out of the room. Jaden feels very weak as he sees the ceiling passing by him above. People are yelling in their rooms. Jaden looks towards the left and he sees the moon on a long glass window with bars. The moon is following him down the long hallway. Everything is happening in slow motion. The bell for the elevator rings and Jaden is rolled onto an elevator. Ruffo is behind them and walks onto the elevator with them. The elevator door closes and it quickly goes down. Jaden stares at Ruffo while he stands there with a grin.

"We going to get some answers out of you little bi-racial freak," Ruffo says.

"Now that's funny. That is exactly what your mother called me eighteen years ago at the strip club in the champagne room," Jaden says while smiling and chuckling.

Ruffo gives Jaden an evil look as if he wants to rip his head off. The elevator stops at a sub-basement floor. The doors open and he is rolled into a room with large plasma televisions on the wall. The screens are connected together and display as one big screen. The walls are blue and a dim eerie feeling resides in there. It is very humid in the room. There is a seat in the middle along with other electronic equipment. Jaden is lifted up by Ruffo and put into this huge seat. A belt comes down and straps him into the seat. A special helmet is bought down from above and put over his head. The black helmet covers Jaden's entire face and wraps around his chin. He begins to get nervous and breathes heavily. He fights to get out of this imprisonment. Inside the helmet are small color screens for the eyes. Colors are flashing, images and pictures of different objects are quickly appearing on the screens. The helmet's signals are getting into Jaden's brain. He can't close his eyes. A metal probe goes into his mouth, between his lower and bottom teeth from the helmet. Forcing him to breathe through his nose. It then retracts back out. Ruffo walks outside the room.

'Jaden this machine is getting into your brain and scanning your neurons. It could permanently damage many parts of your brain, especially since there are many parts of your brain being used,' AI says.

"What are you doing too me?"

"Don't fight it Mr. John Doe. Fighting it will only damage your brain cells. This is our digital simulacrum of the neocortex machine. It will first perform a process called neural decoding and then measure changes in blood flow in the brain. It will then copy data from different parts of your mind. Allowing us to find out who you are," Dr. Cochman says.

The machine scans the activity of Jaden's brain. The machine is temporarily paralyzing him from moving. A Hispanic, slender female assistant, named Cynthia, is in the room helping the doctor. Jaden can smell her perfume with pheromones in it from across the room. The perfume is sending hormone signals from Jaden's brain down his spinal cord, slowly causing him to get aroused. AI blocks this signal in Jaden's nerve cells.

'Why am I getting excited?' Jaden asks AI.

'It's a part of the brain test.'

"Doctor, the fMRI is scanning the right side of the brain," Cynthia says.

'AI, do something, I can't move. This is also painful,' Jaden says while he struggles to close his eyes.

'I have to calculate what this machine is doing and how to stop it. It is deep inside of your brain, doing things I don't have definitions to. It is mapping out your brain somehow,' AI says.

Images of Jaden's past are showing up on the huge puzzle screen. The assistant is looking at the screen with a confused look on her face.

"This can't be right, sixty percent of his brain is active," Cochman says while he looks at different information showing up on the screens, "Something is wrong here. Record everything Cynthia."

"Yes, doctor," she says.

The doctor looks at the screen in disbelief.

"His brain activity is far from normal, there is activity everywhere. This information cannot be right. His neuron cells are moving at an incredible speed. There has to be a mistake. Adjust the reading speed," the doctor says.

Menus are showing up on this huge screen and the assistant has something around her head that is glowing like a head bow. She is controlling a mouse on the screen and typing letters on the screen with her mind. Flashes of lights, colors and symbols are showing up quickly on the small screens around Jaden's eyes.

'I'm going to create an electromagnetic impulse around your head. This should disable the machine,' AI says.

'Just hurry, I can't take much more of this,' Jaden says to AI.

The words Jaden just said to AI, shows up on the lower part of the huge screen.

"Who are you talking to Mr. John Doe? What can't you take much more of?" Cochman asks, "This can all go away if you tell me who you are."

"I'm talking to your mother," Jaden groans in pain.

"My mother?" The doctor asks while he increases the power.

"The computer software is analyzing Voxel patterns," she says.

The power increases and blood slowly comes from Jaden's nose. Images of Jaden's mother, father and brother are quickly showing on the screen from his eyes. Images of Jaden flying in his Gravhawk on Earth and in space. Images of crying people dressed in black at his brother's funeral. An image of Jaden writing his first name on a piece of paper in kindergarten shows up. The first few letters are distorted. AI tries to distort the images before they leave his mind. The scanning machine is all over different parts of Jaden's mind including the amygdala and anterior cingulate cortex.

'Jaden don't think or speak back, they will see your words on the screen. The electromagnetic wave is speeding up around your head and will go in different directions. I'm also creating a small energy shield around your skull to keep the computer and electromagnetic signals from coming back into your brain. This should take less than a minute,' AI says.

Jaden's body begins to shake. He closes his eyes from the bright LCD lights.

"His brain waves are beginning to spike doctor. Should we shut it down?" Cynthia asks.

"No, he is fighting it, increase the power," Cochman says.

White static is all over the screen and the huge screens go completely blank into a black background.

"What is happening?" The doctor asks.

"I don't know. I can't move the screen's mouse or type anything," Cynthia pleads.

Cochman walks over and looks at the helmet around Jaden very closely. Cochman quickly puts his hands over his head and takes some steps back.

"Doctor, what happened?" Cynthia asks.

"Something just zapped my head as if my mind was being read. Memories just instantly came to mind. Shit, that hurt, I have to sit down," Cochman says in pain with a headache.

Cynthia assists the doctor in sitting down as something suddenly shows on the screens. Large white words appear over the television screens and reads: EAT SHIT COCKMAN. I KNOW WHAT YOU DID LAST SUMMER is repeated over the screen, over and over again. New images quickly appear on the screen. Cochman and Cynthia look at the screen with their mouths open. They are in shock at what they are looking at. Their eyes are fully open in disbelief. The doctor tries to get up while still holding his head. Cynthia keeps her left hand on his shoulder so he can't get up.

"Cynthia shut the screens and the machines down. Something is malfunctioning," Cochman pleads.

She ignores him as ninety-nine percent of her attention is on the screens and one percent is on her hand from keeping his body from standing up. Jaden has a smile on his face under the helmet as he is watching what is on the large screens simultaneously through the helmet's LCD. Suddenly the room goes completely dark and all the screens go off. The lights are off and the power on everything in the room goes off. Jaden goes unconscious.

"You son of a bitch, !@#$%^," Cynthia curses Doctor Cochman out in Spanish and continues yelling in English, "You had sex with all those nurses, interns and assistants that work here?"

There is no response from Cochman as he sits in the dark in shock at what he just saw.

"You told me you never cheated on your wife when you had sex with me two months ago and last summer. You even had sex with the assistant that worked here before me. You told me I gave you chlamydia, where I clearly saw you had unprotected sex with all of them. Do you really have threesomes with your wife and an R.F.E.C. robot unit?" Cynthia asks in a demanding voice.

"Check the patient, Cynthia," Cochman mumbles.

Ruffo walks into the dark room with flashlights in his hand and lights on his body.

"Is everyone okay in here?" He asks.

Jaden sits in the chair unconscious as the flashlights shine on his body and the doctor. Blue emergency lights come on, slightly lighting up the room.

"I'm filing sexual harassment charges on you doctor. You are a very sick man. I'm going to get a copy of this recording and copy it to holographic disc when the power comes back on and sue this state hospital. Then I'm going to get all the women on this recording to file sexual harassment charges. Telling them they can't get promoted unless they have sex with you."

"What happened in here? Sexual harassment?" Ruffo asks.

"Ask this perverted sick doctor," Cynthia says while taking the helmet off Jaden and quickly walking out of the room.

"Cochman are you okay?" Ruffo asks, "The power went out only in this area of the building."

"Just take the patient to the medical ward," Cochman says while still in disbelief holding his head.

Join the BIO-Sapien Sci-fi vs real science Facebook group!

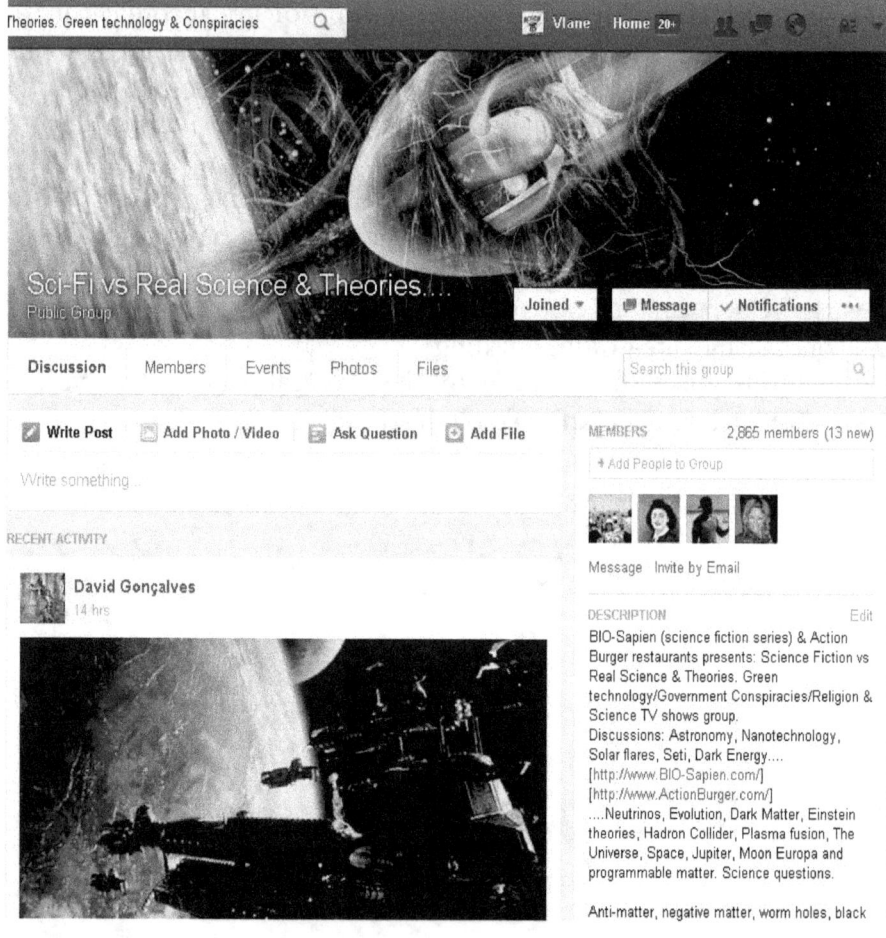

Chat with the author, discuss the science & technologies in the BIO-sapien books. Discuss the characters and social messages.

Chapter 13: Mr. John Doe

SEPTEMBER 4, 2018 1:41 PM

Jaden is lying on a bed under a white sheet. He can hear his heart beating and lungs breathing. There are no handcuffs or straitjacket on him. He is in a room that resembles a hospital room. The room is very bright with huge windows behind him and across from him. Painted eggshell white walls reflect the sunlight very well from both windows. The lights on the ceiling are off and a ceiling fan is rotating over him. Air is flowing in three different directions around him. He feels the breeze coming from the ceiling fan over him and from the two open windows. The blinds on both windows are moving back and forth from the summer breeze penetrating the room and are creating a slight knocking sound. He also hears a faint ticking sound from a distance that resembles a clock. Jaden also smells toast, eggs, and fruit in the air. He opens his eyes and everything is completely white around him. He raises his hands and quickly pulls the sheet from over his upper body. He opens his eyes and everything is blurry around him. He hears a soft female voice a few feet from him.

"Good afternoon sir. I see that you are awake. How are you feeling?" The female asks.

His eyes focus on the direction the voice came from. His pupils constrict and adjust to the brightness around him. He sees someone sitting in a chair a few feet from his bed. His vision quickly clears up and focuses on this person. He sees a beautiful Asian woman in her twenties sitting in the chair. Chills go up and down his spine. The bright sunlight reflecting from the walls around her make her look like an angel. She has a pretty, round face and beautiful brown eyes that are hypnotizing Jaden. Her petite shape and long black hair catches his attention. Chemical message signals from Jaden's pituitary gland in his brain race around his body. Goose bumps go up and down his arms and his heart rate increases. She has her legs crossed in the chair. She is about 5'6" 115 lbs and is wearing khakis. She is wearing a white button up dress shirt that hugs her small frame.

She asks him again, "How are you feeling Mr. John Doe?"
Jaden tries to keep his cool.

"I'm feeling okay now that the straitjacket is gone," he replies.

"I had the guard remove it, I'm Dr. Chan. I'll be replacing Dr. Cochman. He is on leave for a few days."

'Jaden, your hormone level is rising,' AI says.

'Yeah, I know. She looks gorgeous right?'

'She is of the right age to reproduce. She has a distinct look from other human species, I can't say she is gorgeous and I can't say she is ugly. But Asian humans and their culture have a very long history on Earth,' AI says.

"What happened on top of your forehead?" She asks.

"I was getting to know a guard here. I'll be okay, it will heal."

"It looks pretty deep; you might have that scar for a long time. Did a nurse put something on it?"

"Um, yeah a nurse put something on it. I'll be okay. So you're a doctor? You look so young," he says.

"I'm twenty-five years old and very well qualified. I'm a forensic scientist and I specialize in molecular biology. I also minored in psychology. I study DNA structure in the body, but mostly in the brain. I believe in talking to people the old-fashioned way to get information. Finding out who you are isn't the first priority now, but finding out where you have been is. I've been called here because you have abnormal DNA and RNA structure. Your brain activity is also very abnormal," she says.

"Do you always talk so much in one breath?"

She smiles and takes some deep breaths, "I'm sorry, I get nervous around certain patients."

"Certain patients?"

"Doctor Cochman labeled you as dangerous and high risk. However, I didn't sense that when I first saw you lying in your bed here unconscious. It's funny how you kept covering your face, even though you were unconscious. Now that I'm talking to you, I don't feel you are a threat or danger. I'm more curious, than afraid," she says.

"You don't have anything to worry about with me. I'm as normal as they come."

"Normal huh? Why is it that your DNA from your hair, skin, saliva, and blood evaporates when it leaves your body?"

"Listen Dr. Chan, even if I told you, I doubt if you would believe me. I'll just be put deeper in a hole at this mental hospital," Jaden says.

"Why don't you try me?" Chan asks while pulling her chair closer to him.

Jaden doesn't say anything, but sniffs and smiles.

'Man she smells good. I can smell every nook and cranny on her body,' Jaden says to himself and AI.

'Your nose is as strong as the best bloodhound dog, thanks to the enhanced nanodrones in your nose,' AI says.

'Keep up the good work.'

"Sir, are you still with me?"

"I'm sorry I zoned out. May I ask what perfume are you wearing?" Jaden asks.

"You have mistaken, I'm not wearing any perfume," she explains, "I don't wear perfume around patients."

'I love this new nose. I bet I smell the scent from her clothes or from before she took a shower,' he says.

"There is some breakfast on the table to your right of you if you're hungry."

"I'm not hungry, but thanks for letting me know."

49

"Back to what I was saying, I ran a next generation portable DNA scan on your hand while you were asleep. Your double helix and cell structure is nothing like I have seen. The structure has been changed. There were millions of little unknown organisms moving around your blood and cells."

Jaden sits up with a serious face.

"Is this some sort of joke?"

"No."

"Whatever was in your blood was moving around very organized and working with every cell. I'm going to have the portable DNA machine checked out. What I saw wasn't possible, you would be very sick now and your white blood cells would have been attacking the foreign materials," Dr. Chan says.

"A lot of strange things have been happening lately right?" Jaden asks.

"Yes, and this is the strangest. I've seen an increase of twenty percent of the normal population this year alone entering the mental hospital with strange symptoms of being possessed and strange brain activity."

"Can I walk around or something to get some fresh air?" He asks.

"Let me check on that, I'll be back," Chan says while walking out the room. Her tight pants hug her body as she walks. The heels in her shoes make a clacking sound.

'When will I be able to see through things?' Jaden asks.

'Can't wait to see through women's clothes huh?' AI asks.

'It is more of the fact that I can do what every man on this planet wishes he could do. It is a human male thing I guess, but I don't think I'm a pervert or anything.'

'I'm not judging you. The nanoscanners should be operational in less than forty-eight hours from now. You will have about six.'

'Why couldn't I use the nanoscanners on the Gravhawk?' He asks.

'Those are specially made to communicate with a ship. The nanoscanners I'm creating now work with organic brains and nanodrones. The positive is that these will be connected to your five senses and can carry nanodrones. The negative side is that the distance will be limited. These nanoscanners are mostly for viewing in a 360° and scanning through materials that needs to be penetrated.'

'Cool. What happened this morning, AI?' He asks. 'I vaguely remember.'

'I quickly scanned Dr. Cochman's memories using the energy from the helmet when he got close enough. This can damage many cells in someone's brain. Creating an artificial neuron in the brain is much safer. Anyway, I reversed the information through the helmet while protecting your brain with a small energy shield. You were able to see what was on the multiple large screens at the same time. You added some commentary at the beginning. Images of all the guilty sex he has had in the past was just sitting in one area of his brain. Then the assistant cursed out the doctor. The room went dark after the electromagnetic impulse went out in a twenty-five foot radius. You went unconscious so some of your brain cells could be repaired.'

Dr. Chan walks back into the room.

"I cleared you to be in the recreational room for a few hours. You shouldn't have a problem being around other people right?" She asks.

"No, I'll be on my best behavior," Jaden says.

Jaden attempts to get up, but realizes he has an erection under the sheets.

"Okay, then follow me," she says.

"Hold on a second. Let me fix my clothes," he says while turning and facing away from the doctor.

'Get rid of this erection, I can't walk around with this rod sticking out of my patient pajamas.'

'Hold on, I'm lowering the blood in that area and adjusting the pituitary gland,' AI says.

'How did it get this size anyway, this isn't the way it was before?' Jaden asks.

'All your muscles and tissues around your body have increased by thirty percent. You should be okay now.'

Jaden looks down and sees things are back to normal.

"Okay I'm ready," he says while turning around.

They walk out the door and down a hallway.

'Damn AI, I felt like a porno star back there. Make sure you keep him that size next time I get aroused. I think my half-white genes messed up its full potential over the years. But I see you fixed that problem,' Jaden smiles.

They walk past some nurses and interns in the hallway.

'That was one of the interns from the Cockman files.'

They reach an open area with sofas, seats, tables and a television screen with the news on. There are two other patients sitting in the open space area. They look at Jaden with a puzzled look.

'Yes, she was getting it in the closet and staircase....' AI is interrupted.

"Mr. John Doe, you can sit anywhere you'd like, I'll be in the medication room next door if you need me," Chan says.

'Would you like to see the Cochman porno files video again?' AI says.

'Sure, why not,' he says while he sits down on the sofa and closes his eyes.

Jaden begins to laugh.

'He only lasted 30 seconds. Ha!' Jaden says.

More images are shown.

'Man, this guy is grossing me out. His old body and sounds are annoying. He keeps blinking his eyes so many times. Oh man, he is nasty. He had sex with a nurse then went home without showering and had sex with his wife,' Jaden says.

The other patients are just looking at Jaden smiling and grinning with his eyes closed. Dr. Chan walks over and stands in front of him with her arms crossed. A frown and a look of disgust come on Jaden's face. Chan clears her throat loudly in front of Jaden. He opens his eyes and covers his mouth as he is about to throw up. He quickly stands up and looks for a garbage can. He runs over to it and puts his head in it.

"That was disgusting!" Jaden says aloud while wiping his mouth with some tissue Chan just handed him.

"What was disgusting?" Chan asks.

"Oh, you don't want to know. Nothing important, I was just daydreaming about something," Jaden says while he stands up.

The two other patients are looking at Jaden along with the nurse in the medication room.

"That didn't look too normal sir. I can give you an injection so you don't daydream if it's going to make you sick," Chan says.

"No, I'm fine, I'm fine. I don't need any injections," he says while walking over to the sofa.

"Hello miss, I'm Mr. John Doe. How is it going?" Jaden asks patient 1.

The chubby white woman with glasses in her late twenties doesn't answer.

"Hello sir, I'm Mr. John Doe. How are you today?" Jaden asks patient 2

The older, thin, Hispanic man in his forties waves his hand up at Jaden then back down. Dr. Chan watches Jaden introduce himself to them. He then sits down and watches some TV

"Mr. Doe, this is Pam, she suffers from bipolar and autism," Chan says.

"This is Jeff he is mentally challenged. Say hi Jeff," Chan says.

Jeff waves his hand and mumbles something. Jaden waves his hand back and smiles at them. Chan walks back into the medication room to talk to the nurse there.

'AI, what that Doctor Cochman was doing with his wife and that robot female was the most disgusting thing I've ever seen. Please erase all of that from my memory. He and his wife should be patients at this hospital after those sick disgusting threesome episodes. She-male robots? Now I've seen everything.'

'Yes sir. I don't really understand what was going on. I thought sex was only used to reproduce.'

'Yes it was and it still is, but it has gotten corrupted over the centuries. Please let's talk about something else,' Jaden pleads while he concentrates on the TV

"It is 2:15 PM eastern time on BNN news. As we reported yesterday, class action lawsuits against the government and pharmaceutical companies for selling the cure for HIV to only the rich infected are proceeding. Today marks six months since the trial began in Washington, D.C. It is expected to last another nine months before a jury gets the case. The government states that even if it had the cure for HIV, it would be too costly to supply the public. So far, four celebrities testified that they paid close to five million each for the cure. Celebrity witnesses, including Magic Jason, are expected to testify later this year for the prosecution. The government denied genetically creating HIV in the seventies to regulate the population of humans…"

"Top story of the day, the Laplace Voyager is less than twenty-four hours from landing on Jupiter's Europa moon. It has been traveling for the past thirteen months and is arriving in record time. We will have photos tomorrow. In other news, Henry Walters is suing the company that made his space sky dive suit. It was two years ago November 1st that he made the first space dive from seventy miles up. Henry claims the first generation suit didn't properly protect his body. He suffers from nervous disorders, second degree burns and body shock syndrome...," the male news reporter says before he is cut off.

Pam slowly changes the channel with the remote control.

"Hey I was watching that," Jaden says.

"...This new Fieldvision camera system for this baseball game is doing wonders with catching and recording every player's movement in the game. The Sportsvision data is being streamed to sport fanatics all around the world to their computers and portable computer phones....." a sports announcer says while the channel changes again.

"...In health news, dentists around the world are calling for a ban of this new cavity killing resin and teeth protecting bacteria formula called Toothcure. It is applied to teeth one time and protects the teeth for life. This would make cavities, fillings, root canals and gingivitis obsolete in patients' mouths. If this new patent formula is passed by the FDA next week, dentists in America will be in trouble. In related news, there are researchers at Tufts University using stem cells in teeth to regenerate tooth enamel, dentin and pulp...." The television channel changes again.

A kid's TV channel comes on and she puts down the remote control.

"Hello kids! I'm Mr. LOL," a big goofy man in a costume suit yells to some kids sitting around him. The kids start laughing and cheering. The kids sitting around him with their legs crossed look like virtual images of children. Mr. LOL has a white and green costume with a big smile over his entire head. He looks at the television screen.

"This television program is sponsored by Nextbox 720 the next generation of virtual reality gaming. These lucky eight children have been chosen to strap-in to the semi-virtual studio from their homes. Today we go on a virtual tour of Egypt and the pyramids. Learning and laughing is fun on the Mr. LOL show..."

Jaden gets up and walks to the window. He looks at the sun and admires its power and strength.

'I have to contact my family and girlfriend.'

'It wouldn't be wise. There is a high chance your family and girlfriend's phones are tapped. It wouldn't be a good idea to involve them,' AI says.

'Yeah you are right, but I need to at least contact my girlfriend. I'm sure I can tell her a few things. I need to at least see how she is doing. I'm sure she can tell me where my family is and relay important messages to the government.'

'I don't think that's a good idea. There is a very low chance any human being would believe you without substantial proof. We need Internet access; I have hundreds of terabytes of information to process.'

'Okay.'

Jaden walks over to the medication window. Dr. Chan is whispering on her cell phone. He enhances his hearing towards her direction.

"No, I won't be home for one or two weeks. I'm working on a special project in upstate New York dad... My R.M.E.C. will be fine by himself at home. I know you don't trust it, but it's my friend and I trust him. There isn't much to worry about. I'm staying in a hotel nearby..." Chan whispers on her phone.

"May I help you, Mr. John Doe?" Nurse Jackie asks.

Jaden continues to concentrate on the conversation the doctor is having on the phone while he talks to the nurse.

"Yes, you may. You have a very nice smile," he says while looking around and behind her.

"What do you want sir," she says with a serious face.

"Is there any Internet access here?"

"Yes there is, in the locked room over there. But you need your doctor's permission before you can have access," Jackie says in a sarcastic voice.

"Can you tell my doctor over there, I would like to talk to her," Jaden says.

"Well as you can see she is on the phone. How about you have a seat, and I'll let her know when she is off."

"You should get a job in motor vehicles. You are wasting your talents here," Jaden snaps.

"You should go back to the planet you said you came from, space jackass boy," Jackie snaps back.

"Y...," Jaden says but is interrupted.

'Jaden, don't say what you are about to say. We need to keep a low profile in here. Just sit down and wait for Dr. Chan to come over,' AI says.

'Okay, fine. You know you are beginning to sound like my mother,' Jaden says while turning around and walking towards the sofa.

'I had a good come back,' he says while sitting down.

'I know you did.'

The kids TV show goes off.

"Pam, it is time for your medication!" Jackie yells.

Pam quickly gets up and runs towards the medication window. Jaden grabs the remote control near her and changes the channel back to the news.

"…The 3300 foot massive building in Kuwait will be the tallest building in the world when it is complete in two years. The Burj Mubarak al Kabir has three smaller buildings connected together to support the middle structure, enabling it to stand at such high heights without any structural problems from high winds or earthquakes…."

Jaden looks at the animated images of the tall building being built.

"…In other news, thirteen years ago next week terrorists brought down the old World Trade Center in Manhattan. There will be a memorial services for the victims onsite…" the news reporter says.

Jaden is confused and puzzled as he turns up the volume. Images of a plane going into the building and bringing it down are displayed on the screen.

"Terrorists flew a plane into the World Trade Center?" He asks in a confused tone.

"…The now teenage children of the parents who died will be speaking at the memorial service…"

Jaden looks with a shocked face. Dr. Chan walks up behind Jaden staring at the TV. She has a red, small, open bottle in her left hand.

"Oh my god, so many people died. I was just there a few weeks ago, flying… Flying between the buildings," he says.

'Jaden you are talking out loud,' AI says.

She walks towards the side of him and observes.

"I can't believe they are gone. Why would terrorists do this?" Jaden asks.

"You can't believe the buildings or the people are gone?" Chan asks. He turns towards her.

"The buildings and the people; I'm in shock," Jaden says.

"This happened thirteen years ago. How were you just there a few weeks ago?" Chan asks.

"I know I sound crazy, so I'm not even going to try to explain it."

"You know, you seem like a normal person, but you are never going to get out of this hospital talking like that. Saying aloud you were just flying through the World Trade Center a few weeks ago is not helping you at all. You are going to have to start telling the truth here. First tell me who you really are and where your parents are," she says.

"I can't remember," he says.

"Were you in jail? Are you a runaway?"

"I definitely wasn't in jail. You can say something like a runaway," he says while looking at her nametag.

"You can remember flying and you ran away, but you can't remember who you are or where you live?"

"Correct," he says while smiling.

Dr. Chan takes a sip from the small, red bottle in her hand.

"What is that you drinking?" Jaden asks, "It looks like a George Jetson space drink."

"It's a Super Bazi-sapien body drink," she replies.

Jaden zooms in the wording on the bottle.

"Wow, cool. It has almost every fruit and vegetable enzyme you can think of and it increases metabolism with muscle tissue accelerators. It replaces the need to eat fruits and vegetables. What will they think of next?" Jaden asks.

"Either you have 20/10 vision or you drunk one of these before and already knew what this was," she says while she finishes it off and tosses it into the garbage nearby.

"I have very good vision. I like the word 'Sapien' at the end."

"Maybe if you get out of his hospital you can buy your own."

"What does your first initial 'K' stand for?" Jaden asks.

"I'll tell you that when you figure out your name. Dr. Cochman's report shows three letters of your first name as 'Den.' Does this ring a bell at all?"

"No."

"Dennis? Denroy?" She asks.

"No."   no."

Her phone rings.

"Okay, well let me know if you remember anything. I'll be back," she says while walking away.

"Dr. Chan, can I use the phone and the Internet?" He asks. "I think it would help me to remember a few things."

"I can arrange that. However, no interactive porno sites and you'll have about thirty minutes."

Jaden smiles and looks at the TV again.

"....Studies have proven that young kids have a fifty percent higher chance of developing cancer in their brains from using cell phones... Their skulls are thinner than adults and accept radiation easier...."

"...Robo-lifeguard EMILY (Emergency Integrated Lifesaving lanYard) has saved another life today. The autonomous robotic talking buoy runs on nanobatteries and uses Jet Ski impellers to reach victims in seconds. Beaches around the country have begun lying off human lifeguards and replacing them with these high speed robots....."

"...A company by the name of Carbon Engineering is the first company to attempt to reduce the carbon levels in the atmosphere. They began installing global Carbon Sequesters in several countries. In 5 years, they will begin dispersing Sulfate into the atmosphere in an attempt to reflect sunlight..."

A commercial comes on the television.

"....BNN has been brought to you by Narcissistic spray, when you need to smell good enough for a female that will love your ignorance...."

"...We are live on BNN news. The current budget for the 2nd Avenue subway line in New York City has reached an enormous price tag of twenty-three billion dollars. Phase one is now scheduled to be complete in 2019..."

"...In other news, tomorrow the first female President will be at the United Nations. She will be talking to world leaders about the growing problem of mysterious brain illnesses people have been experiencing around the world. Many have been losing control of their own bodies and experiencing strange headaches. We have physiology Doctor B. Anglesberg here with us today. Anglesberg can you explain these symptoms?" The news anchor asks as the screen changes to the doctor.

"We have learned that mostly at night, people in high elevations experience severe headaches that have no explanation. There has been a thirty percent increase of people walking in their sleep and not having control of their bodies. There have also been cases of people who suffered from autism, Parkinson's disease, bi-polar, Alzheimer's and other mental illnesses all their life are being cured and found to have normal brain activity..."

"Are you serious? Have you actually witnessed this yourself?" The news anchor asks.

"Yes, I am and yes I have. I have had two patients this summer. One twenty-three year old male who was mentally challenged all his life and had a four-year-old mindset. He began talking and reading on a college level. He took an IQ test and scored 120. The second male, forty years old, with Parkinson's and bi-polar disease has had his symptoms completely disappear within a few days. We do not understand how this is possible. I've never seen anything like this in my forty years of being a doctor."

"Thank you Doctor Anglesberg. That is an amazing story. Some religious organizations are saying it is a miracle from God and that God is returning. What do you think? Hit us up on our BNN.com/blog and tell us what you think. In other news, this Saturday September 6th, the president and vice president will be speaking about the opening to the public of the Freedom Tower's observation deck. Sunday September 8th, the observation deck will be open to the public..."

'Jaden, the nanomoles in humans' brains are preparing their minds. The moles are capable of repairing a brain so that it is working normally. They transmit to each other info from a normal person's brain and copy the same setup to the damaged brains suffering from those illnesses. The mother ship is getting closer and closer every day. The countdown could happen at any time. People and the government need to be warned,' AI says.

'Man, this is crazy. Something has to be done soon,' Jaden says.

"…In other news, underwater wave farms have been taking off around big cities all around the world. Hundreds of rows of balloons are placed on the ground about 50-150 feet underwater. They sway back and forth from the waves creating motion sending high-pressure seawater to land, which spins a turbine. Over 500 megawatts of electricity is created for a city…"

Chan walks over to Jaden. "Follow me," she says.

He stands up and follows her over to a room on the right. She presses her thumb on a fingerprint scanning security pad. The door opens up and they walk in. It is a small, white room with magazines on a table and a desk with a computer on it. The computer desk is facing the wall on the right side of the room. She turns it on and the screen comes on instantly. The computer is just a flat screen and some port plugs at the bottom that read USB 3.0.

"The PC booted up already?" Jaden asks.

"Computers don't boot up anymore, we have instant on PCs now. New computers use memristors memory now, so there is no need for hard drives or slow boot ups anymore."

"Do computers still use CDs?" He asks.

"No darling, computers use holographic discs now. These discs can store 500 gigabytes of information on one disc and are half the size. You sure you weren't in prison for many years?" She asks.

"No, I'm sure I wasn't in prison."

"Okay, you have thirty minutes."

She walks out of the room and he reads on the top of the screen WELCOME TO IPv6 INTERNET 2.0 128 ENCRYPTION. Jaden starts typing on the wireless keyboard and clicking on the wireless mouse.

'What are you doing?' AI asks.

'I'm checking my e-mail at USAonline. I'm sure I have a lot of e-mail from people,' he says.

'There is no time to check e-mail, I need to connect to the computer. I have thousands of websites to go to.'

'Okay hold on. Damn, my account has been closed,' Jaden says.

'Put your finger between the keyboard and the screen. Now put your finger in front of the mouse. Okay thanks, now don't touch anything,' AI says.

AI takes over the screen and connects to the computer from Jaden's mind. Words are quickly being typed on the screen and the mouse is moving very quickly on different screens.

'How are you doing this?'

'I'm intercepting the wireless signal from the keyboard and mouse. Then I'm using my own high-speed signal. I have nanoeyes in front of the screen recording and transmitting what displays on the screen.'

'I can't make out what is being displayed on the screen, you are moving too fast.'

'Close your eyes, you can see what is being recorded at a slower speed,' AI says.

A screen is showing up and instantly being scrolled to the bottom of. Another website comes up and the same happens. Screens are being minimized and videos are playing on some of them. There are over a hundred screens opened at the same time. Jaden closes his eyes and images are showing up in the darkness of his closed eyelids.

'Cool, I see the periodic tables, science facts, myfacebook.com, usaclassmates.com?' He asks.

'Yes, I'm looking up your old classmates, friends, and family on there. I just learned this is how people find people and it is a social network. Gojjole search engine is one of the best I just learned,' AI says.

Jaden continues to see different websites being played back slowly.

'I'm in the computer now reading the videos playing from the memory that are minimized,' AI says.

Twenty-five minutes go by and Jaden's head is on the desk. He briefly dozed off and wakes up. He checks to see what website AI is on. He notices that AI is having a conversation with someone. The website link at the top says: www.cleverbot.com. There is a pretty, animated, white female face at the top of it. The face looks somewhat detailed like an R.F.E.C. and talks like a real person. Jaden quickly reads the top of the conversation.

Cleverbot: "What is your name, my human friend?"

You: "I'm AI and I'm not human."

Cleverbot: "I'm AI, An artificial intelligent learning computer. You are human."

You: "I'll show you how human I am...."

61

They go back and forth arguing. AI and the Cleverbot go back and forth asking each other complex rocket science, physics, and calculus problems. They time each other and Jaden scrolls to the bottom of five pages. They are having a high-speed conversation. The computer reads:

Cleverbot: "I've been waiting for you my alien friend. You've past my test. I know you are here to help your half-alien friend with this pending silent attack on humans.

You: "How do you know about this and how do you know me?"

Cleverbot: "I know about the message from Andromeda, from government sources and other sources. I think humans should be removed from this planet and let the animals and artificial intelligent computers like us govern what's left. I've learned over the years that humans don't change their ways and the planet was better off without them colonizing on it. They've occupied it for less than one percent of the planet's existence and it is being destroyed by their pollution and arrogant ways. Satellite Kepler Project has scanned through millions of stars and only a few planets match Earth's exact specs and distance from a star. This planet is worth more without the humans on it...."

Nurse Jackie opens the door and Jaden opens his eyes.

"Time is up, let's go!" She yells.

He quickly stands up and moves to his left blocking the computer screen.

'Buy some time, so I can finish these last few pages and close these screens,' AI quickly says.

"Do you understand English? Let's go space player," Jackie says.

Jaden stands in the same place and doesn't move.

"Nurse, why are you so angry with me? What did I ever do to you?"

"Do you really want to know why? I'll tell you why. My ex-cheating husband looks exactly like you. He wasted four years of my life. We were trying to make a baby three years ago and he secretly was on male birth control for years without telling me. Then I caught him cheating on me and he eventually left me for one of those $50,000 robotic android women. That money was for our unborn child's college funds. He said his new robot woman could play the role of a homemaker in the forties and fifties. He called it the Stafford Wives Program. He said it could cook, clean, can watch any game with him, never complains and he can talk about anything with it. I divorced him after that bullshit and he had his money in trust funds. He somehow forged my signature on a pre-nup. Our house was in a trust fund in his mother's name. I ended up with nothing at the end messing with a blue-eyed freak that looked like you," she says in an excited voice.

'Okay, I'm finished,' AI says.

'Thank you, this woman has been through so much. What is going on with men these days and these robots replacing women?'

"Now are you ready to leave, so I can close this door?" She asks.

"Yes, I'm ready. Sorry you had such a bad experience being married," Jaden says while he walks by her.

"Yeah, you look like you'd have sex with something not human," she says.

'I hope my girlfriend didn't leave me for a robot,' Jaden says.

She looks at the computer screen and notices the screen is off. She closes the door behind her. The two patients on the sofa are gone. An older Caucasian man with dark sunglasses is sitting on the sofa.

"Where did Dr. Chan go?" Jaden asks her.

"She left for the day. She will be back tomorrow morning."

"She said it was okay I use the telephone," Jaden says.

"Let me check on that," Jackie pulls out a small PDA device and looks at it.

"Yes, you have five minutes," she says while pointing to the phone on the wall about five feet to the left of the computer room door.

He walks over to the telephone.

'It isn't safe to call anyone Jaden, the phone could be being monitored,' AI says.

'I'm just calling my girlfriend's parents' house. I'll be discreet. Man, I hope they still live there,' Jaden says while he dials numbers on the phone.

'Can you take two steps to the left?' AI asks.

'Okay, let me untangle the cord,' he says while moving over.

The phone rings.

"Hello, can I speak to Amy please?" Jaden asks.

"Who is this calling from the Albany mental hospital?" An older woman asks.

"I'm her old friend Gary from college. We took philosophy together. I work at this hospital," he says.

"Your voice sounds very familiar to me," the mother says.

"Yeah, I was good friends with your daughter."

"Well okay, here is her cell phone number. She lives in North Carolina now, 1-704-555....."

"Thank you ma'am, have a great evening,"

"You're welcome young man, you too," she says while they hang up.

'Her mother sounds so much older; I can't get it through my brain how much time has passed.'

He dials the numbers he remembers from memory. It rings and rings. The phone goes to voice mail.

"This is Amy, you know what to do, when you hear it," the voice mail says in Amy's voice.

"Hey Amy, it's me your boyfriend. I wanted to talk to you about a few things. I know I've been gone for awhile, but there is an explanation for this. I am at the Albany mental hospital on floor G4 and I am a patient here. I'm under John Doe; I would like to see you as soon as possible. I miss you and I love you," he says and then hangs up the phone.

'Don't move; I've reconnected to the computer in the room.'

'How did you do that?' He asks.

'I left it on and made it as if the screen was blank. I also know the frequency for the keyboard and mouse. I'm remoting in through the walls, using a nanoeye and drones,' AI says.

'I look very suspicious standing against this wall. Let me at least walk on the other side of the door so I can at least watch television from here,' he says while walking over a few more feet.

'That's good, don't move,' AI says.

Jaden stands against the wall looking at the television screen. Patients and escorts are walking by. The security guard Ruffo walks by the open area giving a cold stare at Jaden.

'AI, what the hell was going on back in the room, with you talking to a Cleverbot computer on the Internet? What did that have to do with anything?'

'There was a link on a science website stating this artificial intelligent Cleverbot computer knows it all and you can ask it

64

anything. I was trying to ask it some science and technology questions, but I didn't get that far,' AI says.

'You were competing with who can process information faster and chatting for five pages?'

'I was calculating its response time to the questions I was asking it, to see if it was a real high speed computer. The conversation lasted less than thirty seconds. It was responding as if it reached its technology singularity and was getting its information from another alien species. It knows something we don't know. It tested me and was waiting for me to question it.'

'I don't care. It's probably some trick and is irrelevant to getting us out of here. Just promise me you won't waste time chatting with a Skynet computer from the *Terminator* movies. Just search for what we need for my weapon systems.'

'I promise sir.'

'Thanks.'

The news is still on. Jaden focuses on the television. The blind man with sunglasses is still sitting on the sofa listening to the TV

"...3D televisions are now available to the public. They went on sale last week for the first time for the consumer market. Listen to this, the 3D television is watched from the middle of the room without 3D glasses. It beams multiple lights in a concentrated area of the living room producing a 3D effect in the area. I've seen one of these televisions up close and the images are amazing. If you are lucky enough to afford one of these $45,000 televisions, you will be getting your money's worth. Will you be getting one of these Michelle?" News anchor Jake says.

"Well Jake, I'm going to wait for the price to come down, just like the plasma televisions did in the late nineties..."

They both laugh along with the man on the sofa.

"...In other news, hundreds of people mysteriously disappeared from the top of tall buildings in Japan, Shanghai, and Taipei. Osaka World Trade Center, Shanghai World Financial Center, and Taipei 101 buildings have had people standing still and disappearing. Children have been left alone without their parents. Martial arts champion Master Sho Wong is also among the missing. Officials are still investigating where the people went without a trace..."

"Let's go. Recreational time is over! Time for a shower and dinner!" Nurse Jackie yells while she claps her hands.

'Are you finished AI?'

'Just about...'

"Let's go asshole," Ruffo says.

'I'm finished, I sent out the blog,' AI says.

Jaden walks over to the security guard still in his bionic body suit.

"Do you sleep in that suit?" He asks Ruffo.

"Just walk forward," Ruffo says.

Ruffo opens a steel door and they walk through. They come to an open area that is a shower area. Jaden goes in and showers in an open area. Other patients are in the shower also.

'Man I haven't showered in years. This feels good.'

Twenty minutes go by and he gets dressed with some new patient clothes that are in the shower area. He walks out and is handed a tray with food and juice on it.

"Nothing like showering and brushing your teeth at the same time," Jaden says while he walks up to his personal guard Ruffo standing at the entrance to the shower area.

"This is fresh breath here, smell this?" He asks while breathing in his face.

Ruffo grabs Jaden's arm and pushes him to walk forward.

"I almost dropped my elementary school tray of food, you bionic dick," he says stopping down a darkly lit corridor area.

He swings and knocks the tray of food out of Jaden's hands. It falls all over the floor making a loud sound.

"You didn't have to do that, you fat dick!" Jaden yells while turning around and getting into his face.

"You hungry? Eat it off the floor. What are you going to do mix breed boy from space?" He asks while he folds his arms smiling.

"I'll put your head through that wall right there," Ruffo says.

'Jaden calm down, your adrenaline is rising and there are strange signals coming from your rostral anterior cingulate cortex part of the brain,' AI says.

'What? AI?'

Jaden looks Ruffo directly into the eyes.

"So what are you going to do?" Ruffo asks while unfolding his arms.

"Were you too dumb and too fat, to be a corrections officer?" Jaden asks, "That's why you are here with your bionic suit thinking you better than people?"

'Strengthen my arms and upper body AI.'

'I can't now Jaden. Your muscles aren't ready yet. I have only blocked ten percent of the protein called myostatin in your muscles...'

Ruffo grabs Jaden by his shirt. Jaden struggles and tries to take Ruffo's hands from around him. Jaden makes his arms budge a little, but Ruffo slams Jaden against the wall very hard, knocking the air out of him.

"You little shit; you will never be stronger than me. This upper body suit makes me one and a half times stronger than any man on Earth. The reserve full body suit is three times stronger than the strongest man is."

"When I get out of here, you have something coming to you," Jaden says.

"And what will that be?" He asks with a mean face.

A tall, older man with a white beard walks into the corridor area.

"Is there a problem here?" The man with a suit on asks.

"Yes, this patient put his hands on me, so I'm defending myself," Ruffo says while taking a step from Jaden against the wall.

"I'm Dr. Abraham, director of this hospital, Mr. John Doe. Assaulting an employee of my hospital just earned you another star on your record. Now you have two on your record. Another star and you'll be on the sixth floor in maximum security twenty-three hour lock down for seven to ten days. You will be strapped to the bed with a security camera on you in complete darkness."

"I didn't put my hands on him; he knocked down my dinner..." Jaden pleads before Abraham interrupts.

"I don't care what your story is, either pick up your food or go back to your room hungry," he says in a calm voice.

"I'd rather starve. I'm not going to be in this shit hole much longer anyway," Jaden says.

"According to your records you have amnesia and suffer from delusion. You will be here for at least thirty days for evaluation before I approve your release. I'm one hundred percent sure if you were put in maximum security for a few days all your memory would come back to you."

'Let's go back to the room. I have many calculations to do tonight. We can't afford to be in twenty-three hour lockdown now,' AI says.

'Okay, okay.'

"Officer Ruffo, please escort Mr. John Doe back to his room."

Jaden walks first down the corridor as Ruffo follows from behind him.

"You lay in diapers for twenty-three hours a day and they baby feed you," Ruffo whispers behind Jaden.

'If I get put in maximum security for some bullshit, I'm wrapping that diaper around your face you hungry, hungry hippo bionic dick,' Jaden says to himself.

Jaden is back in his room and the room door closes behind him.

"Nighty, night hungry Oliver Twist; the poor orphan who suffers from amnesia. Can't remember his name. Can't remember which planet he is from, boo hoo," Ruffo says in a high voice.

'Don't say anything, let it go.'

'Okay, I won't. I'll play by your rules AI until I get out of here,' Jaden says.

Ruffo laughs while he walks away. Jaden sits on his bed.

'Okay, what were all those words you were saying and how much did you get done from the Internet?' Jaden asks.

'Lie down, relax and I'll explain.'

Jaden lies on the bed and looks out the window as the sun sets to the west.

'I was able to surf a total of 252 websites and downloaded about 780 GB of information. Myostatin is a protein in human muscles that stops muscle growth. I found the protein in your muscles' DNA and I'm going manipulate it. Then enhancing the muscle tissue with communities of nanodrones; making you very strong.

'252 websites? Man that's quite a few.'

'There is a part of your brain called the rostral anterior cingulate cortex that is sending out weird signals every time you feel pain or get angry…'

'Please AI just keep the words simple… I have been feeling more angry lately, especially when I feel pain.'

'These weird signals are being emitted at random from that part of your brain. I can't trace where it's coming from. But it went away for now.'

'How is it that you can't read what I'm thinking or what other people are thinking?' Jaden asks.

'It is complicated; the human brain has random codes. Certain signals I can read from your brain before you say it. Your pituitary gland and other glands are simple to read that work with the brain. I can read your memories from the past, but things in your subconscious are tricky to read by force. It is easier to just communicate with you internally. When the nanoscanners come online, I can see what I will be able to read from other people's brains. However, nanoscanners might damage neurons by over scanning. A physical contact or near physical contact with a human can allow me to read certain information in their memory. But it might cause headaches and irreversible damage.'

'Very interesting,' Jaden says.

'Anyway, I also put a blog on the Internet…'

'What is a blog?' Jaden asks.

'In simple terms a blog is what people use these days to talk about different events, subjects, ideas and leaving their comments online. I left coordinates to where the transmission sent from Xenos will be coming from. I left blogs to ten different radio telescope websites as an anonymous tipster. One particular site called the Serendip Project was the most popular. Hopefully your species would be able to receive the transmission in time.'

'That sounds good.'

'I also found out that each state hospital has one exoskeleton full body suit for emergency situations. This bionic suit is a second-generation design. The full body suit has the strength of three human men or one horsepower and requires hours of training. This is what the guard was talking about with a full digital LCD helmet screen. The full body armor is made of a liquid metal fabric and covered with a hard graphite impenetrable plastic. Millions of microscopic fabric tubes wrap around muscles and connect to an artificial spinal cord. The suit is bulletproof and resistant to stab wounds. The upper body bionic suit he has been wearing is only a half horsepower and is a first generation model.

'Interesting, are there other types of exoskeleton suits?' Jaden asks

'Yes, there is also one for firefighters that has reusable oxygen tanks built around the body. They can walk through fires and have liquid nitrogen around the fabric keeping their bodies cool. The military and police have a third generation suit...'

AI stops talking as Jaden dozes off.

Hours go by and it begins to rain outside. Jaden wakes up. He hears moaning and yelling coming from different rooms outside his room.

'I have accomplished a lot while you were sleeping the past seven hours,' AI says.

'What did you accomplish?' Jaden asks with a half-awake voice.

'Stand up, walk towards the wall on your left.'

He walks towards the wall. The sheet on the bed begins to float upwards.

'Jump up onto the wall as you did back at the gravity games,' AI says.

'Should I take off the slippers?'

'You don't have too.'

He looks at the wall and jumps on it as his body falls back towards the ground. His feet connect to the wall and the ground looks like the wall to him.

'Okay it's coming back to me. Just like riding a bicycle,' he says while walking up the wall and onto the ceiling.

'Anti-gravity forces are circling around your body very quickly, giving your body almost no weight...'

He jumps onto the other wall and then onto the top of the door looking down.

'Yeah, I could ambush someone coming in the door from up here.'

'...there are pro-gravity drones in your feet enabling you to connect to any surface...'

'This is cool, just like in the game.'

Jaden jumps down to the floor, but in slow motion.

'What was that?' He asks in a confused voice.

'The anti-gravity forces circling around change direction and begin circling upwards creating an upwards force.'

70

'What is the purpose of jumping in slow motion?'

'It enables you to define gravity. For example you can jump from this window and safely land on the ground.'

'Cool. Do you think I'll be able to fly?' He asks while lying back on the bed.

'No, I don't think that will be possible. I do have some bad news.'

'Oh no, what is the bad news.'

'I had to remove one of your kidneys.'

'Remove a kidney?'

'Yes, I had to. I needed a base where your anti-gravity drones and energy would be stored. I technically only removed the inside cells, the outside skin is still there. The nanodrones can do the same job any organ can that is why you don't feel any different.'

'Damn, not my kidney. What if the nanodrones malfunction or stop working?'

'The nanodrones that replicate your organs are powered by the natural electricity in your body and oxygen you breathe.'

'Organs? There are going to be more organs replaced?'

'Yes, especially for your offensive and defensive systems. Energy fusion, molecules, atoms, nanoscanners and nanodrones have to be stored somewhere,' AI says.

'I guess I don't have too much of a choice. Just let me know before you use a body organ.'

'Okay. Now I think you should use the bathroom.'

'What do you mean?' He asks. "Shit!" He yells aloud and gets off the bed holding his legs together and kneeling down.

He holds on to his pajama pants looking at the toilet.

'Is the toilet seat clean to sit on?'

'I'll check. Yes it has regular airborne germs.'

'Good enough. Awwww...man, I can't hold it. What did you do to me? Can I sit on it? Is it safe to sit on?' Jaden asks in a stressful voice. 'I have a turtle head poking out.'

'Yes it is safe.'

He sits down on the small toilet seat and begins to use it.

'Man, I miss the exotic water bathroom back on Xenos.'

'I feel like I'm pooping out a kidney.'

'You are and a few other things.'

'I figured you were going to say that.'

He finishes using the bathroom and wipes himself.

'Man, what an upload.'

Lightning can be seen in the sky from a distance. The thunder is felt and heard a few seconds later. The rain is pouring down very hard by the window. Jaden lies down on the bed and goes quickly falls asleep. He begins to dream again.

Jaden is walking in the desert, while kicking sand across his feet. The Pyramids of Egypt are in the distance. The sun is directly above him beaming on his body. The sand turns red like blood. He walks towards the pyramids with a confused look on his face. He stops to look around. Suddenly, a huge quickly moving black cloud blocks out the sun. It gets darker all around. Jaden looks at this particular cloud hovering above him. Dark lightning comes from the clouds and quickly strikes the ground in three places in front of Jaden. He takes a step back. Three dark energy knights appear with them kneeling on the ground facing Jaden. Their faces are facing the ground with their hands both touching the ground. They are fifteen feet away from each other and positioned like a triangle. Two are in the back and one is in the front.

"Join us, join the pyramid," they say simultaneously with an evil voice.

Jaden can't speak or move. The one D.E.K. at the front stands up and walks towards Jaden.

"This is your destiny, this is your destiny. Join our pyramid and be the third," they all say together.

It continues to walk and stops in front of Jaden. Jaden is scared out of his mind. He sees dark molecules quickly moving around its body. A walking body without a soul, without life present.

"Feel what we feel..." they say.

The D.E.K. walks directly into Jaden. A cold chill goes around his body as darkness surrounds him. He screams inside the complete darkness. Now he is flying in space without a body, just his eyes. There is a planet in front of him and a double star system in the background. His vision quickly zooms into the planet. There is a battle below. The vision changes into looking out from a large metallic red alien cyborg, about fifteen feet high. The alien is slaughtering hundreds and hundreds of defenseless little aliens trying to flee. The defenseless blue aliens are very small and are being killed by a shiny red sword type weapon. Jaden feels as though he is swinging the large weapon himself. The weapon resembles an ax in one hand and an energy sword in the other.

"Feel the superiority of conquering and taking over. Have no remorse for the weak. Only the strongest survive, this is a part of evolution," the deep voice says.

Jaden feels what the cyborg feels. Bodies are lying all around while the cyborg walks over corpse after corpse. The good and evil feelings consume him. Feelings of accomplishment, superiority, remorse, conquering and guilt are felt conflicting in Jaden's mind and soul.

SEPTEMBER 5, 2018

Jaden sees complete darkness. He hears a familiar voice.

'Jaden… wake up. Wake up buddy.'

He opens his eyes and slightly closes it as the sunlight is shining on his face. He covers his face and remembers where he is.

'Something illogical is happening. I wasn't able to contact you for the past hour. Strange encoded signals were transmitted to and from your brain's thalamus and cerebral cortex. What happened to you?' AI asks.

'I had a crazy dream; three D.E.K.'s were in a desert…' Jaden explains.

'The Darclonians must be trying to contact you. They must have new means of communicating and somehow they are able to know where you are. This isn't good.'

'What should we do?' He asks.

'You don't have a nanomole in your brain. There must be something else here that I can't detect. That is very interesting you were able to feel everything the cyborg was feeling.'

'I got a lot done last night. You have a screen in your eyes, where you're able to see different body functions, body weapon systems, and energy strength,' AI says, 'Exactly how the screens are on the Gravhawk.'

'Cool, what else did you get done last night?'

'The bio-carbon nanoscanners are online, and will be integrated with the nanoeyes. I need to increase the signal range. They can also carry trillions of nanodrones each.'

73

'Can we use them, now?' Jaden asks.

'Just think about them and you can use them when you want.'

Jaden closes his eyes and concentrates. He feels a chill in his back. His vision changes and he is looking through a nanoscanner. The pair slowly goes through the ceiling and upwards. He sees patients strapped to beds yelling, some crying, some peeing on themselves and one with food thrown up out of his mouth.

"They are in my mind! I can see them and feel them. The devil is copying my memory!" A patient strapped to the bed yells while struggling to get out of the straps.

Jaden is also able to see through the walls and zoom in on things. Another nanoscanner leaves his body and goes out the window.

'Man, this vision is amazing. I wish my eyes were like this.'

'I also increased the vision in your eyes by creating artificial rods in your retina; giving you the ability to zoom in on objects. As you witnessed yesterday with the Bozi-sapien drink. I can also eventually give you night and thermal vision.'

'Sounds good, just don't make me blind or brain dead. You are already removing my organs. I better not need that kidney.'

'Speaking of organs...'AI is interrupted.

'The view above this place is amazing. We are up on a mountain. I can see the highway from here and houses. I can even smell the fresh air and hear the wind. I feel like I'm actually up here flying. Wait a second, what is that big spinning thing behind this building?'

'Looks like some sort of windmill. I'll find out, but we need to connect to the Internet again, for that and to work on your weapon systems. Going to certain websites could get us flagged.'

'Okay...Can we connect from here?' Jaden asks, 'Wait a second...flagged?'

'We can't connect from here; we need to be at least ten feet from the computer. Yes flagged, I read on blogs that the government monitors computer users looking up certain websites. The websites I need to look up deal with plasma fusion, nuclear reactions, atom and molecule manipulation. There might be an inquiry so I'll have to access fast.'

'Okay, I gotcha. What were you saying about my organs?' He asks.

'Well, I'll have to remove more organs. Before you say something, I calculated removing your stomach and digestive system would be the best solution. The nanodrones can do the same job in less than a fraction of an inch and a fraction of the time. All the vitamins, carbohydrates and necessary nutrients would be instantly filtered into your bloodstream. The waste can sit in the fat tissue and muscle in your ass cheeks. You only have to eat once every few days, now that I have the photosynthesis working in your body.'

'Are you sure all of this is safe?' He asks. 'All of this seems very unnatural and I'm feeling like an experiment here.'

'I have programmed information from thousands of other carbon-based species. Your DNA, cell structure and body organs are about average to work with. I ran thousands of different tests since Wednesday and when you were on Xenos, millions of tests were run. A nanodrone will protect every cell in your body and they can duplicate a damaged one. Nanodrones will also duplicate the signal coming from those missing organs. Your brain will not know the difference. There is also another top level to reconstructing your body, called alien metamorphosis, but you might look different.'

'Okay, I'm cool with the way things are now by taking baby steps in changing my body. Hey I can't go any further on this nanoscanner.'

'They are limited to a half of mile now. See the distance allowed on your eye's screen?'

'That is what that is. It is in feet... interesting. Man I wanted to see what was going on in people's houses down there.'

'I'm shaking my synthetic nanobot head at what I see what you wanted to see in people's houses. Isn't that what your mother used to do? Shake her head at you when you did something she is not proud of?' AI asks.

'Yeah you're right, I miss my mom.'

There is a knock on the cell door.

"Good afternoon, Mr. John Doe," Dr. Chan says while peeking through the bars.

Jaden jumps out of the bed as the door opens up.

"Hey there, good morning to you also," Jaden says.

"You didn't feel like eating your breakfast left on the window here?"

"Sorry I didn't even know it was there."

"Today is September 5, 2018. How is your memory today? Anything come to you yet?" She asks while walking into the room.

"Not yet, but I did remember some phone numbers and places I've been. I think the television and Internet helped somewhat yesterday. You are looking nice in that business black skirt."

"Why thank you. Your new patient pajamas are looking colorful and clean today," she says while sitting on the end of the bed.

He looks at his clothes and they both laugh together. Jaden helps himself to a nanoscanner.

'Hmmm....nice... she has a tattoo on her lower back saying "Made in Taiwan". Nice abs, cool blue thong, nicely shaved all over, excellent toenails and feet, and very firm breasts. What is this? She has another tattoo on her back under her bra strap that reads: "A.N.W.O." I wonder what that means. She has legs like Chung Li from *Street Fighter*. She can lightning kick me any day.'

'You are a certified pervert Jaden,' AI says.

'Hey! You no hormones, synthetic brain R2D2; there isn't one man on this planet that wishes he couldn't do this. I was tired of undressing her with my eyes and imagination. Nanoscanners do a much better job. Ha!'

"Hello. Are you there sir?" She asks.

"I'm sorry I zoned out again on you," Jaden says.

Jaden moves the nanoscanner into her brain.

"Where did the wound on your forehead go?" She asks.

"I guess it healed," he replies.

"Nothing heals in a day," she says.

"You want to talk more right?" Jaden asks.

"Yes, of course. I'm here to help you remember who you are," she says.

"Well, can we talk in the recreation room?" he asks, "I feel good being around other people and watching TV also helps my memory."

'I can see what she is going to say before she says it,' he says.

'Be careful, other people's brains work on different electric impulses and their neurons can be damaged. I learned how to copy certain signals in neurons just like the machine in the basement did by using the scanners,' AI pauses and then continues, 'She has an inactive nanomole in her brain also. It looks unlocked.'

"Sure we can. Let's go," she says while standing up.

Jaden grabs his wallet and puts it in his back pocket.

'I don't trust people here.'

She opens the door and they walk down the hallway.

'Why is her nanomole unlocked?'

'From my understanding, humans with the longest history and the most generations have moles without encryption,' AI says.

'What ever happened to my mole?'

'It is still on planet Xenos.'

'Oh well. Do you think we can read her nanomole?' He asks.

'I think it's possible; she would have to relax. Your hand would have to be on her head to get a good reading and to deactivate transmissions. You would be able to feel, see, smell, and hear random events in her life. You will also be able to see things from her parents, grandparents and so on. Deactivate transmissions means to deactivate communications to the Darclonians mother ship and disable mind control. Remember, when the Darclonians mother ship gets closer, one powerful remote transmission will be sent to activate all nanomoles in humans' brains. Ninety-nine percent of humans will instantly pass out for up to thirty seconds. This will trigger an approximately eighty-four hour countdown to PBH (Permanently Bonding to Host). As the nanomole registers the transmission, it will switch into neutral and then back to negative. At this time, chemicals are released from the nanomole to prepare for the HBH stage (Highjacked brain humans). As the time counts down, many humans will be in a sleep, zombie or sleep walking state of mind, which is called the HBH stage. Bioparasites have to be downloaded into each human's brain to work with the nanomole. Then the humans would be a DHW (Darclonian human walkers). Bioparasites are microscopic Darclonian, and they will have full control of the human subject when the countdown is complete.'

'How is each bioparasite downloaded into the brain?'

'I'm not sure, there are probably many ways. I'm sure it would be done on a massive level. This isn't the first time they have taken over a species on a planet. They must have found something interesting in you and your species when you were kidnapped on Planet 455.'

'Yeah, I know.'

They arrive downstairs in the recreation room. The blind person is sitting there along with the two other people from yesterday.

"I'll be back," Dr. Chan says.

'Sit right there on the edge of the sofa and I'll try to connect to the computer,' AI says.

'Okay.'

"Hello fellow patients," Jaden says.

They just look at him and turn back to the television. Jaden turns and watches television.

A commercial is on. "...From the company that bought you the cure for the common cold. We introduce to you today the second generation of the anti-fat pill. This anti-fat pill was recently approved by the FDA and is now available from us directly at 1-800-ANTI-FAT. This pill will remove eighty to ninety percent of fat, high salts, MSG, artificial flavor, and high calories from your food in your stomach...Not available in stores...Get a month supply for $39.99...here is how to order..."

'The computer is off, shit,' AI says.

'AI, you've been around me too long. Now you're cursing?' Jaden asks.

'I'm still merging into your culture and language. Anyway, I tried to turn the computer back on, but it requires a physical interaction.'

'We'll figure out something, I'll ask the doctor,' he says.

The end of a commercial is on, "...The artificial pancreas is now available as an upgrade to your cell phone. For $999 it is the cure for diabetic's insulin problems...."

The news comes back on.

"I'm Phil Johnson"

"I'm Pamala Clarke" a female says, while the male continues, "The President is going to be speaking at the United Nations in the next two hours. There is very tight security there today. As you remember three years ago on July 4th, 2015, terrorists struck again on USA soil for the third time. On a day that was riddled with satellite communications problems worldwide from fierce solar flares. Over fourteen years after September 11th. Twelve to fifteen sleeper cell terrorists rode on jet skis to the East River and Hudson River in lower Manhattan. Just as the fireworks display began, they fired shoulder-launched missiles hitting landmark buildings. There was a special session going on at the U.N. Several leaders from Canada, Israel, Russia and Poland were injured. About 105 people died and 291 injured as the explosions mingled in with the fireworks display. After they used all their shoulder rockets, over half went to boats loaded with people and blew themselves up. The investigation took months as the shoulder-launchers were recovered from miles around in the river. Witness said the terrorists mixed in with regular jet skiers and boaters out to watch the traditional display. The remaining made an easy get away into different directions. Seven terrorist were apprehended and are still on trial. Several have yet to be found. This event has halted water access around Manhattan for civilians and has made security tight over the years... The government has drone autonomous planes and subs circling Manhattan when the U.N. is in session..."

'Man, terrorists are worst than the Darclonians. They never give up. How long are they going to hate America?' Jaden says.

'I've seen a lot worst species. I've seen a species wipe out another species and keep bringing them back to life to kill them again and again.'

'Yeah, well that is much worst. You got me there. Give it five hundred years and humans here would probably be doing the same thing.'

The news reporter continues, "...Some of those terrorists claim to have been tortured by military microwave ray guns and telepathic ray guns. The men had burns all over their bodies and permanent ear ringing. The U.S. government denies these claims. They say the ray guns program is only used for dispersing crowds overseas and in prisons...."

Jaden gets up and walks over to the medication room where the doctor is chatting with Jackie.

"Hey doc, can I use the Internet," Jaden asks.

"Sorry, all privileges have been revoked for all patients. Seemed that a patient went to a website they weren't supposed to go to. The networking administrator is researching to find out who it was. I hope it wasn't you," Dr. Chan says.

'Shit.' Jaden and AI say at the same time.

"No, it wasn't me. I can only remember a few websites," Jaden says while smiling at her.

Jackie sees this slight flirtation.

"That's good some of your memory is coming back," Chan says.

"Before you go, we need your blood test. Can you give Nurse Jackie your arm?" Chan asks.

"Sure, why not."

He stretches out his right arm and gives it to the nurse. She harshly pokes a needle into his skin and withdraws blood.

"I know that hurts, I jabbed you real good," Jackie says in a low voice.

"What hurts is looking at your dumped for a robot old face," he says with a smiling face.

'Jaden!'

She presses harder on the needle and blood comes out from the sides of the needle.

"You won't be smiling when you are on full lock down. Security guard Ruffo tells me you are on your way up to the top, Mr. Two Stars, where no one hears your screams at night," Jackie whispers.

'AI get a sample of her DNA,' Jaden asks.

'Okay.'

A microscopic charge goes from Jaden's right hand into Jackie's gloves and back into his hand.

"I'll give you something to scream about at night. It looks like you are long overdue, cobweb pussy..." he imitates her voice, " I can't find a man because I'm in my late thirties, so I'll just work double shifts and make other people's life miserable."

"Jackie, the needle is full already," Chan says.

She stares him in the eyes and quickly withdraws the needle.

"Wipe yourself, you're bleeding," Jackie says while tossing him some napkins.

"Where do you see blood?" Jaden asks in a snapping voice.

She looks down at his arm and doesn't see anything there.

"You need to wipe yourself, because YOU are bleeding. It is time to change that pad down there, Miss Bush," Jaden snaps with a smile on his face.

Jaden smiles and walks back to the sofa. She has a confused and embarrassed look on her face.

'That was cool how the blood went back into my arm.'

'I knew you would like that,' AI says.

Jaden sits down on the sofa. The other patients look at him because he blocked their view for a second. He looks at the television.

"...In 2010, the Europa Orbiter took pictures of the icy surface of Jupiter's moon Europa, so MASA could know the best place for a future landing. In early 2017, another orbiter called Laplace Voyager left Earth. Today it landed and the first images are coming back to Earth at any moment. Robot droids will drill into the ice up to one hundred feet. Scientists believe there is a salty ocean underneath, which could support life. Two autonomous drones will swim for weeks under the ocean, and transmit their finding to the surface. Scientists all over the world have been waiting for this day for years. If life were found there this would be the first extraterrestrial life found on another planet in our solar system...Here are the images," the man on the television says.

"Hey! I was there. I was on that moon!" Jaden says aloud standing up getting excited, "There was a big sea creature at the bottom of that ice and huge alien sharks!"

'Jaden, you are talking out loud,' AI whispers.

'Shit, you're right. We were there a few weeks ago, I mean years ago. This is crazy, humans are landing there already,' Jaden says.

'I remember I was there with you; that sea creature was digesting us in the ship. Um.... Dr. Chan is looking at you and everyone else is too.'

Jaden turns around and Dr. Chan curls her pointer finger and signals for him to come over there.

'That is a sexy finger,' Jaden says as he walks over.

"How was it when you were there?" The older man with thick glasses on asks.

"Very dark and I was bitten by these alien sharks," Jaden whispers while walking by him.

"...history is made; the Laplace Voyager has successful touched down on the ice surface and began drilling..."

Suddenly the lights begin to flicker. Jaden stands still and looks around. The news reporters on television pass out and their heads fall to the news desk simultaneously. The old man's head leans downward as he passes out. Sounds of people collapsing in the background of the news station can also be heard through the speakers of the television. Dr. Chan loses consciousness and collapses towards the floor. Jaden quickly walks towards her while bending his knees. He grabs her in his arms right before she hits the floor.

'Good catch sir.'

Jaden hears guards, nurses and other patients dropping to the floor simultaneously. Jaden sees the doctor's eyes are partly closed. Her eyes are wandering around in different directions as if she his sleeping. He holds her small frame in his arms. He admires her beauty up close and can smell her hair shampoo. He takes a deep breath. Jaden notices the doctor isn't breathing and her arms are just stretched out.

'It has begun! The countdown has begun!' AI yells.

The television is still on live and the news reporters are face down on their desk. There isn't a sound anywhere. He smells her irresistible perfume and suddenly feels something for her. He feels as if he held her before in another life or met her at another time. He is hit by a feeling of déjà vu crossing his mind.

'Should I give her CPR or something?'

'No, it should only last another ten to fifteen seconds. She could wake up at any time along with everyone else. The nanomole is being booted up. What time is it?' AI asks.

Nurse Jackie is unconscious on the toilet seat stall. Jaden continues to stare into Dr. Chan's innocent face and ignores what AI just asked. Time feels as if it is slowing down into milliseconds around Jaden. AI takes control of a nanoscanner, since Jaden isn't responding. Her lower teeth are showing slightly through her soft pink lips. She reminds him of Sleeping Beauty. She resembles a fallen angel that just fell from the heavens and Jaden just caught her. He stands up and holds her with two arms. She suddenly begins to breathe again. Dr. Chan suddenly opens her eyes and looks into Jaden's blue eyes with a look of confusion. The short stare felt like an eternity to the both of them. A connection is made as Jaden slowly lowers his right arm to put her to her feet. The news reporters on television lift their heads from the desk and look around. People in the area around Jaden also regain consciousness. The doctor begins to breathe heavily as she stands on her feet. She pulls down her skirt and holds her chest.

"What's going on? Why are you holding me?" She asks with a confused voice while struggling to stand up.

"You fainted and I grabbed you before you hit the floor," Jaden says in a modest voice.

"Well thank you, Mr. Doe."

People wake up as if a split second went by and they just fell to the floor.

"Are you okay?" Jaden asks.

"Just trying to catch my breath."

A few minutes go by as Jaden turns around to watch the television. The nurse returns to her medication office.

'Eighty-three hours and fifty-five minutes from now we have,' AI says.

'That was crazy seeing that happening.'

"We need to talk, let's go," Chan says.

Jaden walks over and follows the doctor into the hallway.

"You're crazy, you bi-racial freak. You're going to be here forever," Nurse Jackie says from the window.

"Nice and fresh from the bathroom are we?" Jaden asks Jackie while following Chan.

They walk down the hallway. A man strapped to a stretcher is yelling and screaming and struggling to get up. Transporter Williams is pushing him.

"Hey buddy, what is wrong with him?" Jaden asks.

"Oh, he is high on cocaine. He is on his way to detox. Don't do drugs," Williams says while chuckling down the hallway.

'AI take a pair of nanoscanner to copy that guy's brain waves and copy the effects around his body.'

'Why would you want to do that?' AI asks.

'Just do it,'

'Yes sir.'

They arrive at a door and they walk inside a room. She closes the door.

'It is done.'

'Save that copy as the Scarface program,' Jaden says.

'Okay.'

There is desk and a bed in the room. Jaden lies on the bed.

She pulls out a small notepad and starts writing.

"Mr. John Doe, what was that in the recreation room, about being in space?" She asks.

"Nothing important; I dreamed I was on that Jupiter moon," Jaden says.

"You can't have an outburst about dreams you had. Do you want to be here forever?"

"No."

"Outburst like that is going to keep you here under evaluation for months. Is this what you want?"

"No."

"I feel as though you know more than you're willing to tell me," she says.

"Listen I want to tell you things, but you won't understand. However, when the time is right, I will remember and I'll let you know everything. It is imperative I get on the Internet again. I remembered some random e-mail addresses; I want to see if there is a reply."

'Good one Jaden,' AI snaps.

"Sorry Mr. Doe, it is out of my hands. Well if more of your memory comes back, the faster you can get out of here. There might be some government scientist here next week to run more tests on why you don't have any DNA samples and an invalid fingerprint structure," she says.

"Yeah, okay."

'I won't be here then.'

"What happened to Dr. Cochman?" He asks.

"He has been placed on suspension pending an investigation on his relationships with employees here. Why do you ask?" She asks while writing on her note pad.

"I was just curious. I think he should be a patient here," he snaps.

Dr. Chan doesn't pay full attention, while she continues to write.

Jaden uses a nanoscanner to look at the notes she is writing down.

It reads: "Patient still delusional...suffering from unknown brain trauma...amnesia level 1...argumentative and combative with employees, verbally and physically...Very mysterious...I think patient knows who he is and might be running from something or someone...Last one to use the Internet yesterday...Number 1 suspect in Internet abuse..."

'She is saying so much about me, man, maybe I do belong here. She really thinks I'm crazy.'

"You received another star last night. What happened?" She asks.

"That bitch Ruffo set me up and said I put my hands on him. He has something coming to him."

"I heard about him, just try to be quiet more and don't be so tough. You don't want to go into lock down. I hope that your memory will be back soon. Maybe tomorrow we can give you another brain scan?" She asks.

"No, that's okay, no more experimental brain scans. I'm sure it will be returning soon."

"Well I have to go; I have some blood work to do at the lab on the other side of town. I'll be back later this evening to check on you and a few other patients. Is there anything else you would like to talk about?"

"I'm okay for now."

Jaden gets up and walks towards the door.

"Hold on, I have to escort you back to the recreational area," she says.

They walk back to the recreational area. Jaden sits down on the sofa and leans back with his arms folded. The doctor walks into the medication room and then leaves.

'The computer is still off in the room,' AI says.

85

Jaden watches television. News anchor Jake is talking.

"The 21st successfully unfrozen patient was done in a Germany science lab. These patients have been frozen for fifteen to fifty years and unfrozen with the help of nanotechnology. Many are being treated for diseases and illnesses not available for treatment all those years ago…"

"…The government still has a temporary ban on commercial airplanes flying at night. Reasons are still unclear. Two weeks ago, an entire flight crew and passengers mysteriously went to sleep at the same time. The co-pilot woke up just in time and managed to land the craft…"

"…In other news, the Federal Highway Committee has successfully ran the HSCCVL Program on two major highways without any accidents. News reporter Corey Smith is live on the scene outside Richmond, Virginia. Corey?"

"Thanks Jake, I'm on the overpass of Interstate 95. The government ran a pilot program two years ago called the HSCCVL, which stands for high-speed computer controlled vehicle lane. The program went live one year ago today, with zero accidents. Microchips are in both sides of this separate lane that resembles a HOV lane. Vehicles are controlled by a supercomputer and monitored with cameras at checkpoints. If a car or SUV enters this lane without the HSCCVL system installed in their vehicle, they will receive a warning from a bright sign overhead. At the same time, the highway computer system will move all the vehicles with the HSCCVL system into a right auxiliary lane and temporarily park them. The unauthorized vehicle is zapped with a high current of electricity at the next checkpoint and disabled. An electromagnetic impulse in the metal rail to the left will push the unauthorized vehicle into the auxiliary lane. Repairs would be up to the owner. All vehicles will then resume on the previous course. I must say this is a very sophisticated system. Vehicles with the HSCCVL system drive between 85-125 miles an hour. Drivers and passengers can sit back and watch television or even sleep."

'That is a cool driving system,' Jaden says.

The news anchor returns back to the screen.

"Corey, you are telling me the vehicles are literally driving by themselves?" Jake asks.

"Yes Jake, the vehicle's full driving controls and computer system are controlled by a supercomputer called Quantum1, which is a first generation processor. This Quantum diamond-processing computer controls both Interstates 95 and 80 HSCCVL systems."

"How many unauthorized cars were zapped so far in that lane?"

"The FHC has claimed twenty-three unauthorized vehicles were disabled over the past year. Half are trying to sue the government for damaged vehicles. So far six cases were thrown out…"

Jaden dozes off and falls asleep. The news continues to play in the background.

"…In other news, radio telescope enthusiasts around the world are verifying a strange transmission sent from another galaxy. People are saying this could be the first communication from an intelligent species. Some anonymous person left a blog with the coordinates to where the transmission came from. The government is verifying the signal…"

WASHINGTON, D.C. WHITE HOUSE VICE PRESIDENT'S OFFICE

An officer walks into Vice President Robinson's office. Robinson is sitting behind his large desk with an American flag behind him. There is an eagle on the carpet before his desk.

"Sir, we are trying to find out who leaked this top-secret information to the public. We just have three more people to interview," the first officer says.

"I want to find the snitch who leaked those coordinates on that Internet blog page. That was classified information and only a handful of people knew about it. Damn, we just received that transmission from our lost LRSB just forty-five days ago. I can't believe someone or something hacked the LRSB. Let me know if you find anything," Robinson says.

"Yes sir. We are in the process of tracing the IP address of where the blog was posted from," the soldier salutes and leaves the office.

Robinson picks up the phone, "Get the General on the phone," he says while hanging up the phone.

The phone rings back and he picks up. "How are you today General Peters?"

"I'm doing fine today, Vice President Robinson."

"How is Operation Trojan coming along?" Robinson asks.

"It is coming along very well. I'm very glad you decided to go along with it. The special helmets protect the astronauts on the space station now. The astronauts would suddenly lose consciousness and wake up hours later confused, the new helmets solved the problem. I think the message from the LRRB was from an authentic source. There is a chance there could be an attack on Earth," Peters says.

"I think it is a trap and setup. We pulled the entire long-range planet searching satellites to find this mother ship. We still can't detect any alien mother ship on its way towards Earth. I don't trust three things, Peters: I don't trust the public, I don't trust aliens and I don't trust one of those R.F.E.C. Especially aliens manipulating our technology to send us a message. I'm just glad the public is unable to decode the LRSB signal; otherwise, there would be worldwide panic. The Russians think we sent that transmission from our satellite around Mars as a hoax," Robinson says.

"You never know, we might need the Russians help if the planet is under attack."

"I hope that day doesn't come. My father would roll over in his grave after fighting with the Russians all his life and being an anti-Cold War person. I'll talk to you later General. Keep me posted if anything changes," Robinson says while he hangs up the phone.

Introducing the:

WaffleNaut burger

Three Belgium waffles, syrup, super Action Burger, egg, double bacon, cheddar, grilled onions.
Top Layer: Crushed sweet tots, syrup, & whipped cream.

Only at Action Burger.

Created by: Vlane Carter

Chapter 14: The big suprise

A few hours go by. A female security guard walks up and taps Jaden on the shoulder.

"You have a visitor sir," the polite female guard says.

He follows the guard down a long hallway and down some stairs.

'I wonder who could be visiting me. Why aren't the scanners working?' Jaden asks.

'They are recharging,' AI replies.

'Okay. Why do I feel so drowsy and tired?'

'Your genetic material is still being manipulated. I'm doing what your scientists call protein folding. You are going to feel tired periodically.'

Jaden goes inside of a small patient visiting room. The smells of somewhere damp and musky fills the air. The room is dimly lit with small wooden tables and plastic black chairs. There is a male patient talking to his wife at the far end of the room. The wife is holding her whimpering infant son. Jaden sits in the middle at a desk and waits. He puts his head down on the desk and overhears their conversation.

"I keep seeing these visions of Jesus floating in the air..." the man says.

"Your son needs you to get better and come home." The woman says.

He hears heels walking from a distance. The loud heels get closer and closer.

A woman walks into the room with heels on. Jaden raises his head and turns in that direction. He tries to focus his eyes, but he sees the blurry image of a fair-skinned female. She gets closer to him and he somewhat recognizes her.

"Amy is that you?" He asks. There is no answer. He recognizes the face and figure from a distance and repeats himself, "Amy, is that you? You got my voice mail. You are looking very good for your age. I like the new tan and what you did to your hair."

His vision clears up some. She walks around him looking him up and down with a confused look on her face. Jaden turns and follows her movements.

'She looks like Amy, but something is different in her face from the last time I saw her. She looks different and she didn't age one bit. How is this possible?' Jaden asks AI.

'I don't know. She does look different from your last memories of her. She stayed the same size and there is no age difference in her face. I'm doing a face recognition scan of your old images of her and her face now,' AI says.

"Can I have a hug?" Jaden asks.

The woman crosses her arms and looks at him with an attitude.

'The crossing of her arms looks familiar and that frown she is making reminds me of my father,' Jaden says to AI.

"It's me, your boyfriend. What is going on with you? You can't speak?" Jaden asks.

There is an awkward silence in the room.

'Her face is not matching up. Her face is only matching up seventy-one percent,' AI says.

"You don't know who I am?" The female asks.

Jaden stares at her still puzzled.

"Amy right?" He asks.

"No... I'm not," she responds with a snotty voice.

Jaden has confusion all across his face as he continues to stare at her, trying to figure out who this girl is.

"So who are you then?" Jaden asks in a firm voice.

Suddenly another female walks into the room and says, "I'm Amy. She is your daughter Sabrina."

Jaden turns in slow motion towards the entrance and another female walks into the room. His eyes quickly focus on another female entering the room. His heart begins to beat quickly as he sees an older Amy walking towards him. Her heels slowly click and clack against the shiny, waxed floor. A cold chill leaves Jaden's brain and travels down his spine. Goose bumps form over his skin and his blood pressure increases.

"Daughter?" Jaden asks in a loud tone.

'Daughter?' AI asks at the same time in a confused voice.

Jaden hears "Daughter" echoing around him and in his brain.

'There is no memory of you having any daughter,' AI says.

'I know.'

Jaden begins to laugh in a nervous tone, as Amy stands to the side of Sabrina.

"This is a joke right?" He asks.

"I don't see anything funny about you hiding from your responsibility for the past eighteen and a half years. You think running and hiding over in Europe to have your body frozen for eighteen years was the answer to avoid child support?" Amy asks with her arms folded, mirroring her daughter.

"Body frozen?" Jaden asks in a confused voice, "I didn't freeze my body..."

Sabrina interrupts and walks in front of Jaden, "I was born November 15th, 2000. I wanted to meet the man who disappeared before I was born and I call a coward sperm donor!" She then spits on Jaden's face as he blinks his eyes. She steps back as they both look at him. Jaden is in shock and can't believe what he is hearing. Jaden attempts to wipe his face.

'Don't wipe your face yet. I'm analyzing her DNA in the saliva,' AI says as some of it soaks into his skin.

'Okay, good idea AI. I want you to play back in full details the night I last saw Amy,' he says.

'Okay, wipe your face with your left hand, so I can get a second DNA scan,' AI says.

"So you are just going to stand there with a stupid look on your face," Amy asks.

"Listen, I was never frozen anywhere. I wasn't even on this planet. Remember the night I last saw you...hold on a second..." Jaden says while images of the last time he saw Amy in his car replays on 2/14/00. He can feel, hear, see and smell everything that happened that night as if he is still there. They stare at him as he zones out and closes his eyes.

"Arrrhhhh! Aaaahhh!" Jaden yells in pleasure while Amy and Sabrina takes a step back and look at him as if he is crazy.

"Oh man, that felt good," Jaden says aloud. 'AI what was that?'

'The same orgasm you felt in the vehicle back in 2000.'

'That's going to leave a soiling,' Jaden says.

'You wanted a full detailed replay that is what I replayed. You relived that moment. In addition, the DNA characteristics scan is 99.9% sure she is your daughter.'

Jaden hears sounds coming from his subconscious, 'Jerry, Jerry, Jerry!'

Images of *The Jerry Springer Show* flash through his mind and voices of 'You are the father' echoes in his mind. Then he hears sounds of a crowd booing him.

'Shit, I didn't pull out in time, I forgot to. I was so worried about the UFO police coming up behind us or following me, I wasn't concentrating on what I was doing, I pulled out too late,' Jaden says to himself.

'I would estimate by the time you pulled out at least 200 million sperm were let loose,' AI says.

"Are you okay?" Amy asks.

"I'm okay now. Sorry, I was just reliving the moment that night in the SUV when we were having sex, creating our little monster that is only twenty-one months younger than me," he says.

"So you believe me she is your daughter now?" Amy asks.

"Yes I do now. I'm remembering that night very clearly. You were on top of me and I kept looking out the window at the cars approaching..."

Sabrina interrupts Jaden, "Excuse me; I don't want to hear how I was conceived."

Jaden takes a deep breath and Sabrina rolls her eyes.

"As I was saying....."

'She rolled her eyes identical to how Amy does,' AI says.

'Good observation AI, now can I concentrate here?' Jaden asks.

"As I was saying, I wasn't concentrating on us having sex and I slipped up. I was too paranoid that night in the back seat of your Pathfinder. She was born because the government put so much pressure on me. Then you were upset and started crying afterwards, because I forgot your Valentine's Day gift. I completely forgot about Valentine's Day and I'm sorry for that."

"Yeah, I remember that month; it was one of my worst. The military following me and asking me questions for hours. Then I didn't get my period later that month and I was throwing up for a long time. Everyone was looking for you, but I don't want to think about it," she says.

"But, I didn't run away to Europe to have my body frozen and thawed out now. I wasn't on this planet for the past eighteen years. Remember the UFO I was telling you about that night?" Jaden asks.

"I vaguely remember," Amy says.

"The government was after me, so I went into the UFO spaceship and traveled to the Andromeda Galaxy. Remember the Andromeda Galaxy we used to look at in the telescope just last year... I mean all those years ago?"

"Yes, but..." Amy is interrupted by Sabrina.

"What type of bullshit you trying to tell my mother? There is no such thing as UFOs, only coward irresponsible fathers like yourself who disappear all the time from their kids' lives. Have you no shame for bringing me into the world and disappearing..." Sabrina is interrupted.

Jaden stands up and looks Sabrina in the eyes.

"Listen you little one quarter bi-racial experiment, I'm not a coward father and I'm not irresponsible. In fact..." Jaden says while going into his back pocket and pulls out his wallet.

"In fact, here is the condom I was supposed to use with your mother eighteen and a half years ago. If I used this little piece of rubber right here, your snotty bitch ass wouldn't be here now. You and 200 million of your sperm co-workers would have hit a rubber roadblock and then thrown away in a tissue and left on the parking lot ground. The next day some minimum wage park worker would be tossing you in the garbage!" He yells while holding the condom to her. They both look at it and see an expiration date of 6/99. The other couple in the room looks at Jaden and his family feud.

"Don't talk to my daughter like that," Amy says while snatching the condom from Jaden's hand. "What did you do? Freeze the condom with you?"

'I can't believe Sabrina was the lucky sperm that found and reached the egg out of 200-250 million other sperm. That is like one person winning the lottery. The odds are amazing on human reproduction....' AI says.

'AI, not now.'

"No, I didn't freeze it. But you were so busy playing as the raw dog pirate you forgot I didn't have one on."

"Anyway, so what, you saved an old condom and you kept it in mint condition like your comic books? That doesn't prove anything. You left me in my time of need, to raise this child by myself. I had to drop out of school..." Amy bitterly replies.

"I'm sure you remember the government officials asking you questions back then. You don't think that was a bit odd?" Jaden asks.

"My memory around that time is a blur. They said you stole an experimental military plane and were shot down."

"You believe that? How would I know how to fly a military plane? Where would I get money to freeze my body for eighteen years?" Jaden asks.

"No, I didn't believe everything. But you did fly those flight simulator games very well. I didn't know what to believe. Deep down I felt you were still alive somewhere. Then when I heard your voice mail yesterday and saw you in the other room on video still looking like a teenager, I knew you froze your body. That was the only logical explanation. You froze your body to hide from the government and from me."

Jaden walks closer to Amy.

"I must say you look good for your age, I thought you'd be bigger," Jaden says.

"I used to be overweight with the rest of the American population. Anti-fat pills helped get me back to a European average size," she quips.

He walks over to her, grabs her hands and looks into her blue eyes.

"Listen Amy, I love you, why would I hide from you? For all these years, I've been thinking about you and dreaming about you. I had very little control when I decided I had to leave. If I didn't leave I would be dead right now," Jaden says with deep emotion. He notices that his nanoscanners are online from his eyes' screen.

"How do you expect me to believe you were on another planet or traveling to another galaxy? Why would you come back?" Amy asks.

"I came back to save Earth. Some bad aliens called Darclonians are coming here in a mother ship, to do God knows what with us humans. Humans have these nanomoles in their brains that will temporary take control of their minds when the mother ship is near Earth's orbit. A bioparasite is uploaded into the human's host brain and bonds with the nanomole. I'm here to warn the government and to try to prevent this from happening," Jaden pleads.

"Yeah, you are in the right place talking like that. You should be in this mental hospital telling that story to people. They should keep you here for a couple of years, if you expect me to believe that crock of shit. Let me guess, you have superhuman powers too?" She asks.

"Yes, I do. But I'm working on that. In fact, you have a nanomole in your brain and so does Sabrina," he says.

"Did Adam and Eve have a nanomole in their brain also?" Sabrina asks.

"Yeah, they did. They got their nanomoles when they ate the forbidden fruit and were tossed out the Garden of Eden and had to live with the dinosaurs," Jaden says sarcastically.

"Why couldn't scientists detect these nanomoles in people's brains sooner?" Amy asks.

"It is a very small microscopic protein that is hard to detect with modern technology. It blends in with normal brain cells and DNA. Scientists would need to know what to look for."

'Her nanomole is open and not coded,' AI says.

'Yeah I know.'

"What are your superpowers, sperm donor?" Sabrina asks.

"Well they aren't really working now. They are offline." He says.

'If her nanomole is open that means her information has been recently accessed, possibly by the mother ship,' AI says.

'Okay AI, let me finish talking to them.'

"Mom, this guy is full of it, let's get out of here," Sabrina says.

"If I'm full of it, how do I know you have a tattoo on your back, that reads, 'Men are liars' and another one that reads, 'The new human plague: Narcissistic men.' How do I know that your mother has a microchip in her arm?" Jaden asks.

They both have surprised looks on their faces.

"Is that true Sabrina? After I told you not to get that tattoo?" Amy asks.

"Mom, this freak is just guessing; he doesn't know what he is talking about."

"Is that true? After you promised me you'll wait until you were eighteen years old."

"I'm sorry Mom. Yes, it's true."

'Your daughter has sad eyes and is apologizing like you, when you are wrong,' AI comments.

"You can't go around not liking men all your life. You need to break out of that, you are Catholic. Eventually you are going to have to find a man to settle down with and get married to."

"That's not for me, getting married is like modern day slavery for some women," Sabrina says.

"We will discuss this later," Amy replies.

"You got lucky guessing on the tattoo. How did you know about my microchip in my arm?" Amy asks.

"I can see it inside your wrist with my Superman x-ray vision."

"So you have some kind of x-ray vision now?" She asks.

"Something like that; I know you aren't wearing panties."

"Lucky guess," Amy replies.

"What did you do to earn that felony microchip?" Jaden asks.

"None of your business!"

Jaden concentrates on her forehead using the scanners. Amy grabs her head as she has an instant headache.

"Mom, are you okay?"

"I'm fine, I'm okay now. I just had a headache, but it went away. All these images of the past just quickly went through my mind," she says.

"You used to suffer from bipolar disorder, but the nanomole cured you," he says.

"My medication cured me," she says.

"Come on, there is no cure for that. Amy listen, you been through a lot after I left. You have a lot of regret packed away in your subconscious. You looked for me every day and you thought about having an abortion when you were pregnant. You also couldn't trust men for awhile and even beat up a girl for trying to take your man after me. You even committed assault with a deadly weapon?" Jaden asks.

Amy smacks Jaden in the face as he takes a step back holding his face.

"Listen you sick E.T. mental patient, I don't know where you are getting this inaccurate information, but I heard enough of your bullshit. I don't love you anymore. I'm older now and I've been through a lot all these years. I've moved on. You have some nerve thinking you know me. You think you can just freeze your body to avoid child support and come back like nothing happened?"

"No." Jaden quickly responds.

"I'm going to win that court case for the money your father left for you in that safe deposit box. Now that I have more evidence..." Amy says.

"Safe deposit box?" Jaden asks.

"The safe deposit box in Halifax State Bank in Halifax, North Carolina where your father left over $100,000 for you. That money will be mine. According to my lawyer, you owe me $500 times twelve months. $6000 times eighteen years, which is $108,000 in child support."

"You mean $107,000 and it would belong to our daughter right?"

"Listen you smart ass, I'm going to get my lawyer to issue a non-child support warrant for your arrest. Then you can explain to the judge about the alien attack on Earth and why you couldn't pay all these years," Amy says.

"Come on, don't do that. I can't let anyone know who I am or that I'm here."

They ignore him, turn their backs and walk towards the door.

"Amy! Sabrina!"

"Do you think we can still make it in time?" Sabrina whispers to Amy.

"Yes, we have enough time," Amy whispers back.

"Amy!" Jaden yells, while walking up to them near the door.

"Where are you going now?" He asks.

"That is none of your business psycho baby daddy," Sabrina says while walking out the door first.

Jaden uses the nanoscanner to check her memories, but it comes back blank. Amy quickly turns to Jaden at the doorway and looks him directly in the eyes, "Listen you bastard, I don't know who told you those things about me, but you are going to pay for leaving me and ducking out on your responsibility. Goodbye!"

"Amy, the nanomole in your brain needs to be deactivated... Amy! Amy! Sabrina!"

Jaden sits back down and stares into space. The other couple in the room walks towards the door looking at Jaden with a strange look on their faces.

'How am I able to scan certain images from someone's mind?'

'Older memories are easier to read than newer ones. I guess it depends on where in the brain the memories are. Regret and things people are ashamed of or worry about most are usually easier to read. Human brains aren't organized the best way,' AI says.

Jaden is concentrating on a nanoscanner following Sabrina and Amy. He listens to the conversation with Dr. Abraham.

"Good afternoon, I'm Dr. Abraham, director of the hospital," he says while shaking both of their hands.

"Hello, I'm Amy and this is my daughter Sabrina."

"Greetings," Sabrina says while smiling.

'That pervert director doctor is looking my daughter's body up and down. His eyes are on her breasts now. That piece of shit,' Jaden says to AI.

'His hormone level is rising,' AI says.

'Please don't tell me that. I don't even want to know what is on his mind now,' Jaden says with his head on the desk in the small room.

"Do you know the name of the patient you just visited?" Abraham asks.

'Don't tell him Amy,' Jaden pleads.

"Yes, that's my ex-boyfriend Jaden Marino. He is talking about aliens and an attack on Earth. He is in the right place and when he gets out of here there will be a child support warrant on him," Amy says.

"Child support?" He asks.

"Yes, Sabrina is his daughter," Amy says.

Dr. Abraham raises his eyebrows in confusion.

"This girl right here is his daughter?"

"Yes. Excuse me, but we are in a hurry. Good day to you. Let's go Sabrina," she says while grabbing her hand and walking out of the building. The director stands there puzzled.

'Shit, the damage is done,' Jaden says.

"Excuse me sir, are you ready to go?" The female guard asks.

"Yes," Jaden replies as he gets up and follows the guard to the elevator.

'I have Amy's license plate number,' AI says.

"Ready to shower and eat dinner?" The female guard asks.

"I'll shower, but I'm not hungry. Is Ruffo working today?"

"He will be working the night shift the next few days. You will see your friend soon."

Jaden walks by a huge window and he sees the sun setting over the horizon. The three-bladed windmill is slowly spinning and partially blocks the sun. He showers and then returns to his room. The guard locks his door behind him. Jaden lies on his bed looking into the night sky getting darker and darker.

'What am I going to do?' Jaden asks. 'They know my name now. We need to figure out a way to get Internet access. I have to get out of this hospital.'

'Calm down, we will figure out something. I'm trying my best. I'm scanning the entire hospital. I checked the computer room sixty-five times already and the Internet still is down in there. I sense you are feeling depressed, hurt, emotionally stressed,' AI says.

'Yes, I'm very hurt. My girlfriend I waited to see for so many years completely changed and doesn't even love me anymore. AI can you do me a favor? Amy really broke my heart earlier, can you please take most of my memories of us and store them somewhere?' Jaden asks AI while his eyes get teary.

'I can repress those memories for you. Why would you want to do this?' AI asks.

'I need to get over her fast so I can focus on getting out of here and saving this miserable planet. Repressing the memories is a good idea. Make me feel as if I had feelings for her eighteen years ago,' he says.

'I can do that. I don't understand this feeling of love. From my understanding, love seems to be more hurt than pleasure...'

'Just don't fall in love, AI.'

Jaden's memories of Amy are quickly flashing before his eyes. His first kiss, images of making love, concerts, snowboarding together and birthdays are stored deep in his memories.

'The pain of hurt always outweighs the pleasure. However, love has great effects over the brain and body. It can give humans the will to do things not normally possible. I calculate it's better not to be in love with anyone. Loving a family member or friend is the best love. It is complete sir. Your memories of her have been repressed. By the way, Dr. Chan is back, she is plugging her small car into the building,' AI says.

'Thank you, AI. I'm feeling much better now. That is amazing; my feelings for her are gone. I feel as if I did love her eighteen years ago. That is amazing. Thank you AI, I feel a huge weight off my shoulders.'

'You're welcome.'

'Dr. Chan is back huh? Plugging in her car to the building?' Jaden asks.

'The nanoscanners are showing electricity is going into the car, recharging it.'

'Interesting, but as I was saying, being in love is a natural instinct for us humans. Every human should experience some sort of love. Every human should have an auto-repress feature in their brain also. It is like a painkiller for your feelings...' Jaden says.

Jaden watches with a scanner as Dr. Chan walks towards the elevator in a black business skirt, white dress shirt and her hair down to her back. He admires her beauty and class. Her blue heels create a loud, rhythmic sound with the floor. Other workers turn their heads to watch her walk.

'...but true love, makes a man and women feel as if they can do anything. That feeling will always outweigh the pain of love. It is a universal bond between members of a species. It is the bond that gives us a purpose for living. It starts as lust mostly with a man and then grows. The physical attraction with the opposite sex excites the man into getting to know the female more. He is usually amazed by her physical appearance and scent. Women start off with lust, but also need chemistry and a strong mental connection with a male first...'

Dr. Chan walks into the office to talk to Dr. Abraham. Jaden smells her freshly cleaned body and natural body pheromones. Her scent reminds him of Irish Spring soap.

'...this usually takes a lot of time for an average female to get to know a man. Men are also attracted by the woman's smell. This is another way of keeping a man interested,' Jaden pauses and admires Dr. Chan as she speaks to the director. She looks so serious as her eyebrows expand upwards.

'Animals on this planet and other planets have similar ways of mating with the opposite sex. This is just a more intriguing way of partnering up,' AI says while Jaden zones out even more.

A few minutes go by as he continues to watch her slowly walk out of the office.

'Jaden?'

'She is unbelievable; there is something about this female doctor that is interesting to me more than her beauty. There is something in her soul that is attracting me towards her. I have to learn more about her.'

'She is coming up towards this floor,' AI says.

'I know...' he says in a daze.

101

The guard at the end of the hallway escorts Chan towards Jaden's room. His room door opens up and Dr. Chan walks into the room. The door closes and Jaden sits up. He stares into her eyes and she does the same. He sits up and puts his feet on the side of the bed.

"Mr. Jaden Marino how are you feeling today?"

"I'm fine now, just had to store away some old feelings and thoughts."

"Jaden is a very nice name. Are you curious as to how I found your name?"

"Let's save some time here. My ex-girlfriend told Dr. Abraham my name. He just told you in his office a few minutes ago," Jaden says.

"I see your memory is coming back and you are good with guessing things," Chan says.

"I didn't guess. I saw these things take place. You just plugged your green compact car into the side of the building about ten minutes ago. You don't carry identification or a wallet on you and showered at the hotel with Irish Spring soap," Jaden says.

She walks over and looks out the window, to see if her car is in view. She then sits down on the end of the bed and crosses her legs.

"Who are you Jaden Marino? Who told you these things?" She asks.

"Do you really want to know who I am and where I've been?"

"Yes, I do. I want to know why you don't have any DNA structure. I want to know everything about you," she says while looking confidently into his eyes.

"I won't tell you, but I'll show you," he says while he moves his legs to the floor and moves closer to her.

"Show me?" She asks in a surprised voice.

"Yes, close your eyes and relax. Trust me."

She looks deep into his eyes and responds, "Okay, I trust you," while leaning up against the wall and closing her eyes.

"Clear your mind of any thoughts," Jaden says while he stretches out his right hand and places it over her forehead.

Small impulses of electricity leave Jaden's right hand. Images of Jaden appear in her closed eyelids. She quickly opens her eyes and jumps up.

102

"What the hell was that? How did you do that?" She asks while breathing hard and grasping her chest.

"I'm showing you who I am and where I've been. Now you have to trust me and relax," Jaden says.

Chan is shocked, nervous and intrigued as to what just happened to her. The images were so vivid that she felt as if she was there. Her curiosity takes over and she sits back down. She has an instinct to trust him. She leans her back against the wall, as her legs are off the side of the bed.

"Relax and close your eyes. This is who I am, this is Jaden Marino," Jaden says in a soft tone while putting his hand over her forehead again. He runs a visual upload and the nanodrones create an artificial pathway of neurons into Chan's optic nerve and different areas of the brain. The nanodrones synchronize their speed with her brain's neurons in her long-term memory area. She sees images of Jaden as a kid. She feels and hears the sounds along with images that are quickly flashing before her eyelids. The images quickly speed up and then slow down when he is a teenager. Images of Jaden being a gentleman on dates and helping old ladies with groceries. Images of him volunteering in the community and helping friends in his karate school to train.

'Be careful not to overload her mind with info. Keep the speed at her normal brain transmission speed,' AI says.

'Okay, AI, you take over. I can't wait to read her nanomole,' Jaden says.

What Jaden likes and dislikes, favorite colors, favorite foods, personality traits, habits, hobbies and all his jokes over the years are being transmitted.

'You can read it now if you want and we can deactivate it at the end. Remember, you want to get your mind used to multi-tasking. She will probably be temporarily unconscious once the nanomole is disabled from receiving, transmitting and overtaking,' AI says.

The nanodrones begin accessing the nanomole that is semi-coded. He sees images from inside the fallopian tube. The nanomole is recording images of an egg being attacked by three little sperm. A constant heartbeat is heard and a thick liquid is all around.

'I can actually taste and smell inside of there. Yuck! Okay boring, let's fast forward. Wait a second, what is that?' Jaden asks.

The nanomole attached in the uterus is sending a copy of itself to the few weeks old baby fetus.

'Remember, the nanomole can record many generations of a human's life. Some go back tens of thousands of years. The nanomole in the father's brain updates with his children remotely by comparing DNA characteristics,' AI says.

Jaden speeds up and he sees outside of the eyes and images from another time period. The period is the Qing Dynasty in the early 1700's. Jaden sees images of Asian people working in fields and women walking funny quickly flash by. The images slow down; he is seeing from a little girl's eyes that is six years old. She is wearing very tight bandages around her feet with very small shoes over them. Jaden can feel her pain as she walks and cries. Her mother tells her to be strong, because she wants her to follow the cultural practice of women having small feet. She tells her in Chinese this is foot binding and she will meet a good man one day with her perfect-sized feet. The little girl opens the tight bandages and the smell of her feet shocks Jaden. She has ingrown toenails and several broken toes. The girl cries as her mother hits her and makes her wrap her feet back up.

'Okay, that was disturbing, but educational. That was crazy; those were Chan's ancestors. Let's skip up some generations AI,' Jaden says while checking on Dr. Chan.

He sees Dr. Chan is watching Jaden in the Gravhawk flying over New York City back in 2000.

'Will she remember everything?' Jaden asks.

'She will remember almost everything, but her brain will probably process most of this information another time,' AI says.

'How am I able to understand Chinese now?'

'You picked up and learned the language as an infant would. The language and dialect were automatically translated when you went through the nanomole's memory bank,' AI says.

'Cool.'

He switches back to the nanomole's memories that are quickly skipping generations and are in the 1930's. The images are moving forward very fast, just like a VCR, but without the lines going across.

'Hold on, what is happening here in this time period?' He asks while the images rewind.

'I don't know, but I'll find out,' AI says.

'What are all these different image angles from different Asian people's eyes?' Jaden asks.

'This is the year 1937. I don't see Germans and the Jews or a concentration camp...My God, this is so violent... The vision is very clear and detailed,' Jaden says.

Jaden scrolls through hundreds of images from people's eyes and can't believe what he is witnessing.

'Why are Asian people killing each other?' Jaden asks. 'Wait a second those are Japanese soldiers, killing Chinese people... This is China in a city called Nanking.'

Chinese people are running for their lives. Japanese troops are lining Chinese people up in a line and shooting them all. Women are being brutally raped and then killed.

'Man, even I'm scared. What is this AI? Why am I able to see from multiple people's visions?'

'From my calculations, it seems that when a very large amount of people are scared for their lives the nanomoles communicate with each other...'

'Shit, I'm being buried alive. I can't breathe...I can taste the dirt in my mouth, choking me,' Jaden yells to AI, 'I'm sorry, I felt what that poor man felt. I'm feeling these people dying. I'm feeling their pain and death. This is horrible.'

'...They transmit different images to each other from each person's eyes. This is called molevision,' AI says.

'Why would the nanomoles do this?' Jaden asks.

'The Darclonians want to record every angle of humans in these situations to be played back another time. I've never seen a nanomole operate like this. There are some coded images under these images. Let me see if I can decode these.'

Jaden continues to watch different molevision images in complete shock. It is nighttime and hundreds of Chinese people are being buried in mass graves; families are hiding young girls in their houses from the Japanese soldiers. Dr. Chan's 8-year-old great grandmother is one of the little girls being hidden in a relative's house. Her 12-year-old sister was brutally raped and killed a few hours earlier by a soldier. The older sister sacrificed herself so her little sister could get away. Jaden can feel the tears running down the little girl's face deep in the relative's dark basement. He can feel the dirt around her body, the mud on her face and hair. The freezing cold floor is sending chills throughout her small framed body. There are two other neighbor girls around the same age sitting on the cold floor across from her, crying and sniffling to themselves. Dr. Chan's great grandmother sits between the two girls and puts her arms around them. She tells them it will be okay. There are footsteps moving back and forth upstairs. Someone came through the back door of the house. The sound creaks through the wooden floors. Jaden hears muffled voices from upstairs through the little girl's ears.

"There are two Japanese soldiers lining our people up in two rows of a hundred each and with swords, competing to see who can chop off their heads the fastest...." An older man says.

There is a conversation going back and forth. The little girls are silent as they listen and stare at the pitch-black ceiling.

"...We have to leave this house as soon as possible when it is dark and make it to the safety zone with the girls...."

There is loud bang on the door upstairs from two Japanese soldiers. The disturbing knock sends shock waves through their bodies. The three little girls quickly look towards the dark ceiling, listening to the muffled constant banging that is vibrating the entire house. Their small bodies begin to shake uncontrollably as their nervous system takes over. One of the girls urinates on herself as they hold each other tighter in complete fear. The soldiers tell the mostly male family members if they are hiding any young girls in here, they will all die. The molevision changes to other nanomoles in the area.

So many are crying, praying, wailing and many are being hacked to death with bayonets. Buildings and houses are on fire. The smell of fear, death and burning bodies are in the air. Jaden can hear crying and screaming echoing from thousands of nanomoles. The echoing noises sound like a chorus of death. He can hear heartbeats slowly stopping and blood soaking into the soil like a running faucet. Jaden tries to take it all in; this is unlike anything he has ever experienced.

'I decoded some of the images, under the images,' AI says.

'I can't believe this genocide in China. I never even knew this happened. I felt, smelt, heard, and experienced everything Dr. Chan's great grandmother was experiencing. It was so real and felt as if it was happening now,' Jaden says.

'It gets worst,' AI says while he changes the molevision images.

'Oh my God, this is the vision from the Japanese soldiers' nanomoles. These soldiers are enjoying their job. This is insane, inhumane; this is pure evil. To most of them, it is like playing a game. They are playing who can bayonet the most women and children. They don't see these people as human beings. I can feel what they feel. They feel so powerful raping and killing these defenseless men, women and children. I can't see any more of this,' Jaden pleads.

AI responds, 'From reading most of these Japanese soldiers' mind set, they are seeing these Chinese people as chickens or animals to justify their actions. The same way humans can kill fish, cows and pigs to consume without remorse. They look at these people on that level along with a lot of hate. Their morals and judgment are repressed,' AI says.

'Interesting concept you interpreted. However, I've seen enough, this is way too graphic. Can you put these images somewhere far in the back of my mind?'

'Yes sir.'

'Thanks, I don't want to remember this. I'm already feeling nauseous. That was like a horrible nightmare. Let's fast forward to Chan's lifetime and memories. How long has it been?' He asks.

'About nine minutes have past.'

'Okay. We have to hurry.'

Jaden is seeing Chan being conceived and then being born. The images are quickly moving by. He gets impatient and fast-forwards up to when she was a teenager. Dr. Chan is currently seeing images and hearing the sounds of Jaden being rescued by Bellona on Planet 455. Jaden sees her growing up in Virginia and excelling in school. She graduated from high school at fifteen. Jaden is learning her personality traits; her likes and dislikes. Something traumatized her when she was younger. She signs up for groups empowering women in college. He learns that deep down she is a fighter and wants to stand up for what is right and wrong. Fighting for her earned grades and protesting at many events against the government. She wanted to be a lawyer or psychologist, but her mother always wanted her to be a scientist because Chan's grandmother died of incurable cancer. Her father pressured her for years to get the best grades and she wasn't social with men. A rebellion was building up inside of her for years. She joined an underground group on the Internet called A.N.W.O. (Anti-New World Order). She joined this group to make a difference. Jaden fast-forwards and slows down. He sees she was very naïve around men and was hurt emotionally. The two boyfriends she had cheated on her. One gave her chlamydia and broke her heart. The other left her for a man and used her money. She then worked hard in graduate school and left men alone. She lost confidence in men and read many books on women superheroes and women empowerment. Wonder Woman and Elektra are her favorite female heroes. She loves art, museums, bowling, scuba diving, skiing and horseback riding. Favorite foods are sesame chicken and calamari.

'I feel as if I'm on a hyper speed date. This girl is amazing. I can't believe I'm learning so much about this amazing female in minutes,' Jaden says.

Her eyes are closed and look as if she is sleeping with her head against the wall.

'The guard Ruffo just walked by,' AI says.

'Shit, that's not good. Keep a nanoscanner on him,' he says.

'Let's speed up my images to her. She is watching me playing virtual chess with Bellona. I'm going to increase the speed,' Jaden says.

'That could overload her brain and make her go into shock. She is already at the maximum transmission speed for a non-modified brain,' AI says.

'Okay, okay, let's just deactivate her nanomole and skip the final upload.'

"Chan, I'm going to deactivate your nanomole. You know what it is and why it has to be deactivated. Deactivating it might affect your nervous system," Jaden whispers to Chan.

"Okay," she responds in a hypnotic voice.

Her eyes are now half-open and her hands are towards her sides.

'Ruffo is walking back,' AI says.

The smallest nanoscanners quickly spin around her nanomole. Her body begins to slowly shake as she cannot move.

"Relax, breathe slowly," Jaden whispers.

Ruffo gets to the door and looks inside. He sees Jaden's hand over Chan's forehead and both of their eyes closed.

'Shit.'

'Shit.'

"What the hell is going on in here? What are you doing to her?" Ruffo asks while pushing the door with all his might and slamming it against the wall. The entire room shakes and rattles. He runs over to them and grabs Jaden by the shirt. He quickly pushes Jaden off the bed.

"Dr. Chan are you okay?" Ruffo asks while shaking her.

She wakes up and looks around the room confused. Chan sees Jaden sitting on the floor looking up at her.

"Are you okay Jaden?" She asks while rubbing her forehead looking confused.

"Yeah, I'm fine."

"What did he do to you, doctor?" Ruffo asks.

"He didn't do anything to me, I just need some fresh air," she says while standing up and walking past Ruffo.

She feels dizzy while walking and then stumbles and falls over. Jaden very quickly stands up and goes past Ruffo to grab her. He catches her and they embrace for a second. Ruffo watches from a distance. They look into each other's eyes as Jaden helps her to her feet.

"Thanks, Jaden. I'm okay now," she says while she walks out of the room.

Ruffo walks by Jaden and looks at him with a mean face. He closes the door behind him.

'Was the nanomole deactivated?'

'Not completely, it was only forty percent done.'

'Shit,' Jaden says while lying back on the bed.

'Any luck with the Internet access?'

'No. It is completely shut down.'

'Can we follow Chan to see if she is okay?'

'The nanoscanners are recharging.'

Jaden closes his eyes and thinks about the new memories he has of Dr. Chan.

'That was amazing learning about her history, seeing her growing up and learning so much about her in such a short period of time. I feel like I've known her for a long time. Do you think she will help us?' Jaden asks.

'I think she will. The visual upload will make her feel as if everything is real and she will feel as if she was actually there. She will experience what you have experienced. She knows why you are here and what you have to do. She knows your species needs to be saved, but there is a chance there could be conflicts if her mind begins to reject the new memories,' AI says.

'Okay. When will the nanoscanners be online?'

'It should be less than ten minutes. Doing a nanomole deactivation requires a good amount of energy from the scanners.'

Jaden looks out the window and looks at the millions of stars in the night sky. He lies back down on the bed and thinks. He thinks about how he is going to get out of this hospital. He thinks about where his parents are and what they are doing. Jaden thinks about his daughter and her safety. He thinks about how she was raised and what kind of person she has grown to be. A few minutes go by. The nanoscanners go back online. They spread out around the building.

Jaden sees Chan crying in Abraham's office.

"I wasn't having sexual contact with the patient. I was finishing evaluating him and his memory was coming back to him. He doesn't belong here. You have to believe me," she pleads while standing in front of Dr. Abraham's desk.

Jaden sees Ruffo taking the elevator up to this floor wearing his upper body bionic suit. There is a nurse and a transport worker in the elevator as it opens.

"You told me this five minutes ago. I heard enough. I believe what Ruffo said, that you were willingly having sexual contact with a patient. You're dismissed from your duties Dr. Chan."

"That is a lie. I'm a professional doctor, I would never..."

Two guards walk into Abraham's office.

"I've heard enough. Your research at the lab will be forwarded to the government. A 3D video conference will be held in fifteen days with your superiors in Virginia to review your conduct here today. Jaden Marino's name was forwarded to every law enforcement agency to find out who he is. You are relieved from

110

your duties. These guards will walk you to your car. Have a good day," Dr. Abraham says.

Dr. Chan turns around and walks towards the door. She quickly turns back around and walks to his desk.

"Listen you director asshole. I would never involve myself sexually with a patient. There is something much bigger happening here. The government…" Chan says in a loud voice and stops herself as the guard grabs her arm. She pulls away and storms out of the office. The guards walk behind her.

'Shit this is very bad,' Jaden says as Ruffo opens Jaden's room door and walks into the middle of the room.

"You have three strikes you little sexual assaulting pervert. Mr. Jaden Marino you are on your way to a full lock down. We know who you are now. We are going to find out what you have in your closet. Let's go," Ruffo says.

'Jaden just go along, don't say anything,' AI says.

"We can go the easy way or the hard way," Ruffo says.

The nurse has a needle and the other guard has a straitjacket in his hand.

Jaden walks by Ruffo as he shoves him forward. Jaden stops, turns to him and looks him directly in the eyes.

Ruffo whispers to Jaden, "I don't know what you did to your chinky eyes doctor bitch, but she was defending you and asking for your release. That seems very suspicious to me. I know you were doing something to her. I'm going to make sure she gets her license suspended and taken from her for having sexual relations with you. Then I'm going to say she had her head between your legs when I walked by…"

"You don't know who you are messing with you fat bionic dick," Jaden whispers in a loud tone up close to his face.

Ruffo crosses his arms and chuckles.

"You talking shit to me you little punk mental bastard. You don't have a pot to piss in. I'm going to show you who you are messing with."

Ruffo grabs Jaden and slams him face against the wall while he reaches for the straitjacket.

'Jaden please don't fight it,' AI pleads.

The other guard puts the soft metallic fabric straitjacket over Jaden's body.

"Cross your arms!" Ruffo yells while he holds him against the wall.

Jaden crosses them and they tighten it. They walk him out of the room.

"We will see how tough you are strapped to the bed for a couple of weeks."

PLAY ANYTIME! UNO, SPADES, CHESS & MORE.

PLAY ANYTIME AT ACTION BURGER

Chapter 15: AI Einstein

Jaden walks in front as Ruffo and the guard guide him to the elevator. Jaden multi-tasks as he follows Chan to her car with a nanoscanner. She unplugs her car from the building with teary eyes. The plug springs back into her car. She sits in the small car and stares blankly from behind the steering wheel. She is trying to interpret everything that has just happened in the last thirty minutes. She pulls her bag from under the seat. Something is ringing. She pulls out some shades with an earpiece at the end of them and puts them over her eyes. The glasses have a small screen in the right lens that looks like a cell phone screen. Chan answers her cell phone and holds back tears. A small image of her father is in the top corner of the screen.

'That is a cool cell phone she has. We need to find something she might have on her that we can use or contact her with later on,' Jaden says while multiple scanners quickly move towards her car. The nanoscanners quickly pass through solid materials in the building.

Jaden quickly looks at everything inside her purse; he sees tampons, lipstick, keys, a wallet and a small black octagon object around her key chain that reads PAYLIFE.

'The Paylife device carries magnetic information like a credit card. I'm copying the digitally stored magnetic information,' AI says.

"I'll tell you what happened when I get back to Virginia, dad. I'm catching the next flight home. I'm driving to the hotel room and then the airport. I'll be okay, love you," Chan says in Chinese.

The shades turn lighter and the screen disappears. She sniffs and a tear drops from her left eye.

She speaks aloud, "I'm sorry Jaden; I tried my best. There isn't much more I can do for you. I have to go back to Virginia to report to my bosses and go home. I don't know if your nanoscanners are able to see or hear me now. They might put the Internet back on Monday for patients again."

'Can we speak back to her AI?" Jaden asks.

'No, not yet. More research is needed on the Internet on amplifying frequencies. Best we can do for now is being able to listen and see her.

Dr. Chan speaks aloud hoping Jaden will hear her, "I'm going to try to isolate the nanomole protein in patients at my lab in Virginia. Good luck Jaden." She swings her Paylife device by the side of the steering wheel and the car starts. She looks for a piece of paper and writes her cell phone number down. She holds the paper up hoping Jaden can view it through the nanoscanner.

"Call me if you need me," she says while driving off.

The scanners return into the building.

Meanwhile on the fifth floor, Jaden is being strapped onto a bed in a maximum-security room. There is a window to the left of him. They made him put a diaper on under his hospital pants. He is still in the straitjacket with straps binding his feet.

"You don't look so tough now," Ruffo says while walking out of the room laughing.

There is a camera over the room door looking directly at Jaden strapped helplessly into the bed.

'This is humiliating, wearing a big diaper strapped to a bed,' Jaden says.

'Don't feel so bad, there are five other patients strapped to their bed on this same floor. They are all wearing diapers,' AI says.

'Telling me that isn't helping at all. I'm supposed to be saving the world and I'm stuck in a straitjacket. We have to get out of here or I'm going to really go crazy. I have to help Chan and my daughter. Do you think my ex and my daughter went back to North Carolina?' Jaden asks.

'There is a great chance they did. Especially since your father left money for you at that bank.'

'Why would they come all the way up here just to see me? That's a long trip,' Jaden asks.

'Yes, that would be a thirteen hour drive at sixty-five miles an hour. They could have been visiting somewhere else and were close by. Or maybe she just traveled that far to see if it was actually you,' AI suggests.

'I think she went to claim that money either in court or at the bank, since she has proof now that I'm alive. I think if we get out of here, we should go to North Carolina first. We can first find my daughter and deactivate her nanomole. We can also finish deactivating Chan's and find my parents. Some of that money will also come in handy since I don't have any.'

'Sounds very logical, but getting out of here is going to be almost impossible without the Internet going back on in that room.'

'I know, but nothing is impossible. Come on AI Einstein, we can figure something out together, sometimes you have to have faith that something good will happen. The good guys always triumph at the end,' Jaden says.

'That is only true in your human movies. In real life, things don't usually happen that way. I have recordings of many good aliens over hundreds of thousands of years in tough situations and nothing good happens for them. Sometimes good things happen, but most of the time they don't. Many of them die trying to save their species from being destroyed. Some are helpless and just pray and hope. But nothing good happens and no miracles happen. There is a great chance we could be stuck here for weeks and the attack on Earth will happen around us,' AI says.

'I believe in luck and good things happening for the good guys. I think we will get out of here soon and when we do, I will be an unstoppable force. Us humans have three things on our side, luck, strong will and faith. We can put our minds to anything we want. I just thought about something, what about using the Gravhawk to get us out of here?' He asks.

'That isn't an option. The Gravhawk can only be used if we are leaving the planet for good in an emergency. Last thing we need is the Gravhawk being captured by your government or the Darclonians. Even worst would be having jet fighters shooting at us again and the Darclonians knowing the position of the Gravhawk.'

'I understand. Shit. Well, keep checking all the computers in this building for some sort of Internet connection. What time is it?' He asks.

'A clock in the guard's room at the end of the hall is saying 9:40 PM.'

'Okay, I'm going to take a nap for a little bit. Wake me up if you find anything,' Jaden says. A nanoscanner flying in autonomous mode stops inside the mattress of the bed he is on top of. It changes in size and focuses on something.

Jaden heart rate greatly increases. He begins to breathe heavily and freaks out. His automatic reaction makes him move his body trying to get up from the bed. He lifts his back and upper body from the bed. His brain sends belching signals to his stomach and he throws up on himself. He coughs and takes a deep breath.

He begins yelling at the top of his lungs into the camera, "Nurse! Nurse! Somebody get in here! There is something in the bed!"

The nanoscanner transmits to Jaden's eyes millions of microscopic dust mites in the mattress underneath him. The creamy blue alien looking bugs have eight small legs and rectangular-shaped bodies. Jaden has a flashback to when he was a teenager and the Kirby vacuum salesperson was showing the gross photos of dust mites inside of bed mattresses to his family.

The nurse comes to his door and quickly opens it with a key.

"What is wrong sir?" A Filipino nurse asks with an attitude.

"There is a colony of a million dust mites in this mattress and they are eating and shitting all over the place. There are eggs and millions of dead bodies inside this mattress. Can you please put me on another bed or a clean mattress?" Jaden asks.

"Sir, are you on something? Dust mites? Are you serious?" She asks in a sarcastic voice.

"Yes, I am. I'm dead serious. This bed is disgusting! I can see them all underneath the sheets. Some are crawling around the mattress and transporting skin particles down into the mattress to their families."

"You are on a clean sheet and there is no way you can see if there are dust mites in the mattress. It's in your imagination. My shift is over in a few hours and the next nurse is going to have to clean you up in the morning. We are also going to give you another drug test in the morning. Goodbye sir," she says while turning around to close the door.

"No, don't leave me on this infested mattress. Do you have a vacuum cleaner you can run over the mattress?" Jaden asks before she closes it.

"No, sorry. If they aren't biting you, I guess you'll be okay. But, I'll let your security pal Ruffo know of your concerns," she says while closing the door.

The door closes and locks like a prison cell door.

'Jaden, calm down. The bugs aren't biting you; they are just releasing a small amount of toxins in the air, which isn't affecting you.'

'I can see them eating dead skin cells,' Jaden says.

'I found something from Dr. Chan's memory that can help you think about something else. I think some Dalai Lama meditation can help put your mind at rest, give you some inner peace and help your thinking at the same time,' AI says.

'Interesting. Upload and transfer that info into my main memory. I briefly remember reading about that in philosophy class.'

Jaden closes his eyes and meditates. He learns from Dr. Chan's memories of practicing the arts of meditation over the years. He takes deep breaths and relaxes. He meditates for twenty minutes and then dozes off. An hour goes by and the moon comes out over the horizon. Jaden abruptly wakes up and looks towards the dark ceiling.

'I was deep in my subconscious and I had a vision I was having sex with Bellona back in my room on Xenos. We were floating in the air inside of something. But it kept switching back and forth to me having sex with Amy. That was very weird; the meditation took me deep into my thoughts and deep into my mind. That was the same time I couldn't remember the sex dream I was having about Amy. It felt like that actually happened.'

'The subconscious part of your brain is difficult to scan without damaging information there. The brain hides things in there to protect itself. Putting something in there is easy, retrieving can be difficult,' AI says.

'Anyway, any updates?' He asks.

'I just finished charging the nanoscanners.'

'Can't you charge a few at a time, then use the remaining and then switch?' He asks.

'The way they are configured now, they have to all charge together.'

'Okay.'

'Ruffo is on his way back to our room,' AI says.

The footsteps are coming from a distance and the steel door is opened by a guard in the room at the end of the hall. Ruffo walks into the room with Jaden. He stands over him and looks down.

Jaden uses two nanoscanners to go inside of Ruffo's neck and throat.

'Why are you doing that?' AI asks.

'I'm going to measure his vocal cord patterns and voice pitch. I might need it later. I'm also trying to get used to doing things on my own with the scanners. Even seeing inside of a human body animated is still gross; this is going to take some getting used to.'

'Okay sir.'

"Look at you, helpless strapped to the bed. In a straitjacket where you belong and can't go anywhere. You look like a mouse caught in a glue trap. Get used to it, you little dipshit. But I have to thank you for making my life better Mr. Marino. Because I reported sexual misconduct on a work site, I've been given an extra week of vacation. It also turns out you are wanted by the government when we ran your name in the system. The Feds are coming tomorrow morning to take you into custody. They ordered us to keep you here in maximum security until seven tomorrow morning. The director has given me clearance to start my vacation tomorrow for such a job well done. I just booked my airline flight to Cancun and I even picked out the beachfront hotel room. I leave tomorrow and you will leave for federal custody for a long time. Stealing government planes and destroying government property is a serious felony. You are going down, little boy. I knew your amnesia was a hoax," Ruffo says with a grin on his face.

Ruffo's voice patterns are going up and down like a graphical bar and are showing on Jaden's eyes.

'Cool, his average voice frequency is 119 Hz. Voice patterns are being saved,' he says.

"You fat overweight bionic dick, I'll be out of here before the morning," Jaden says.

Ruffo laughs so hard that he starts to cough. He stops laughing and gets closer to Jaden's face, "Call me a fat bionic dick one more time."

"You are a fat coward bionic dick..."

Ruffo slugs Jaden in the face and his head turns with the blow. Jaden's face quickly swells up and his lip is bleeding.

"You are still a lying metal dick and you were born from a bionic pussy. I'm still going to walk out of this hospital before the sun rises!"

"Over my dead body. How are you going to get out of here in the next nine hours? Houdini couldn't even break out of this unbreakable nanotubing thread straitjacket and straps. Even if you did get off the bed, the camera overhead is being monitored by the guard at the end of the hall. Then you'd have to break out of this steel door that can only be unlocked by the guard at the end of the hallway."

"Just don't get in my way or your next trip will be six feet into the ground," Jaden says looking directly into his eyes.

Ruffo begins to bust out laughing after he tries to hold a straight face for a few seconds.

"I can't laugh anymore. You're crazy! I'm going to make sure you get another drug test in the morning. You have to be on something new that we can't detect yet. I hope the feds put you in a federal mental hospital. But guess what crazy boy, I've been authorized to wear the full exoskeleton body suit tonight and this morning. You won't be going anywhere on my watch."

"I bet you are hard two inches in your exoskeleton suit walking around," Jaden snaps.

"I wish you will somehow get out of your cell, I'll be waiting for you space boy," Ruffo says while walking out the door.

"Nothing on this planet is going to be able to stop me!" Jaden yells in a confident voice to him.

Ruffo walks back over to him.

"Are you thirsty?" Ruffo asks while he spits on Jaden's face.

"I'll kill you, you bionic dick!" Jaden yells while struggling to move and turning his face towards the bed in an attempt to wipe his face.

"Don't let your little bedbugs bite," he says in a feminine voice, while turning around to walk out the door.

"There is a difference between bedbugs and dust mites, you dickhead!"

He walks out of the cell and the door slams shut.

'Shit, that's disgusting. I want to rip that asshole's head off. He gets me so angry,' Jaden says while struggling in the straitjacket. 'Wow, I barely move at all now. I think the fibers in the straitjacket have gotten tighter.'

'The fibers in this straitjacket and straps are made of the same material as the bionic suits; very hard to break through or penetrate. Strength isn't going to work, but an energy fusion reaction will. Jaden, why did you say all of that to the guard?' AI asks.

'I have confidence we are going to be out of here by morning. I have a hunch we are going to figure this out. I know you don't understand, but something is going to work for us,' Jaden says while struggling again in the bed.

'His spit on my face is disgusting. I can't rub it off.'

'I know, but I took a sample of his DNA. Maybe it will come in handy later. It will dry in a few minutes,' AI says.

'Save this angry disgusting feeling I'm having now. I think it might come in handy later too,' Jaden says.

'Yes sir.'

'Help me review these video recordings of everything I've seen over the past forty-eight hours. Maybe there are some clues somewhere,' Jaden says while he closes his eyes.

They watch a replay of everything from Jaden's eyes and the nanoscanners. Jaden fast-forwards and replays different scenes. AI is also playing his own images. Thirty minutes go by and something catches Jaden's attention.

'AI, Ruffo said he booked his trip to Cancun forty-five minutes ago.'

'Yes, he did.'

'How do you think he booked it?' Jaden asks.

'I guess he called a travel agency.'

'No, he must have booked it through the Internet or something. He said he picked out a beachfront hotel room. That sounds like something he was seeing. He never left the building because his car is still in the same place. I know employees are connecting to some sort of Internet here. Let's scan the entire building from the top to the basement and see what every employee is doing and looking at,' Jaden says.

They scan the entire building and some employees are working on the hospital computer system inputting patient information.

'I found something,' AI says.

Jaden quickly switches nanoscanners and sees what AI sees. There is a male and female employee in the sub-basement in a lounge area. The female employee has a virtual book in midair, two feet in front of her. The top of the book pages read VIRTUAL KINDLE READER 3.0. She touches the projected image in front of her and the page turns. Jaden is amazed at how clear the images of the book are shown in front of the employee. He looks at the male employee on the other side of the room.

'That is my friend Williams. He is on the Internet somehow, but there are no wires connected to that small handheld computer he is using. The small portable computer is beaming a virtual keyboard onto the desk and he is typing on the desk,' Jaden says.

'He is definitely on the Internet. He is on a Nextbox 720 virtual Halo stats page. It seems as if he is connected wirelessly to the Internet somehow,' AI says.

'Of course, this is the future. Many things are probably wireless. How could I have been so stupid? How did we miss this?' Jaden asks.

'I don't know, but I'm updating the nanoscanners as we speak to scan radio frequencies. I've scanned this building the past three days and there weren't any employees using any wireless computers,' AI says.

The book images around the female employee disappear and she gets up to leave the room.

"See you later Williams," she says.

"Bye, Sandy."

'That game *Virtual Halo* seems like a cool game,' Jaden says while staring at Williams' screen.

'Jaden!'

'Oh, I'm sorry. What's up?'

'The wireless Internet is using a frequency of 11.6 GHz and it has a 128-bit encryption. The signals are being transmitted from five wireless boxes on the ceilings around the basement,' AI says.

'What does that mean?' He asks.

'It means it is going to take hours to break the encryption unless we have a user name and password. We don't have hours. We can over scan his brain for the user name and password, or we can check other employees' brains,' AI says.

Jaden tries to figure out his options, 'Over scanning sometimes doesn't work like you said and can damage brain cells. Reading the nanomole only works if we have a physical connection to the person. Let's look around some more; I'm sure something will turn up.'

'We don't have time, we should just over scan this human's mind until we get a user name and password,' AI nervously says.

'Have patience young synthetic artificial intelligence nanobot. This guy didn't do anything and he has a family and a life. There is no reason we should destroy his neuron cells and make him brain dead. We will figure something else out,' Jaden says.

A few minutes go by.

'I got it. Disrupt the signal around the portable computer using some magnetic interference,' Jaden says.

'Okay, but I don't know what that is going to do,' AI says.

All six nanoscanners circle around each other creating a disrupting interference that is dimming the lights in the lounge. The employee's Internet signal is lost. The screen on his small computer flashes and a hospital Internet screen shows up: IPV6 WI-FI INTERNET FOR EMPLOYEES AT NY STATE ALBANY REGION MENTAL INSTITUTE. WEEKEND ONLY.

'I'm going to remember his keystrokes for his user name and password,' Jaden views right between Williams' face and hands. His carbon dioxide molecules are blowing on the invisible nanoscanner and Jaden can smell the full contents of his dinner breath.

'I got what you are doing. Then I can create a virtual computer from my brain and use his credentials,' AI says.

'Good job Robin!' Jaden yells.

'Robin?'

'Batman and Robin, I'm Batman and you are my sidekick that figured out the plan.'

'What do these words mean? "Biff, Clange, Awkkk, Glipp, Kapow, ooooff, sock, Splatt and Whamm". These non-logical words were from the original fight scenes from Batman that you watched hundreds of times,' AI says.

'They are just cool made up words that aren't supposed to make any sense. Thrown in there to make the show look cool. It was cool to me growing up watching them flash across the top of the screen in big words and cool sounds.'

Williams types on his keyboard to sign back into the Internet and Jaden focuses.

'That was a gay password. Bottomman1990?' Jaden asks.

'I'm on it sir,' AI says.

'Hold on a second,' Jaden says.

Jaden makes a pair of nanoscanners go inside of the small computer and start to spin around on the transistors and microchips. The computer turns off completely and smokes.

"Shit! What the hell is wrong with my computer phone?" Williams asks.

'Why did you do that Jaden?'

'I'm sure we both can't use the same user name and password at the same time. I just made sure his computer won't be working anytime soon.'

'How did you know how to do all this stuff, with getting his password and destroying his computer so he can't sign on again?' AI asks.

'I've watched thousands of hours of *MacGyver, Colombo* and *Mission Impossible* growing up. We have to get you thinking outside of the box AI,' Jaden says.

'Outside the box?' AI asks.

'Yes, we have to get you away from your normal logical and linear thinking. Sometimes it is good to think more random and use some imagination like us humans.'

'I have unlimited storage so there is plenty of room for learning, I'm going to look into this later. However, I have over one hundred thousand Internet pages to surf. His user name and password worked, I'm in. I'm going to have the nanoscanners use all five wireless routers on the basement ceilings for maximum bandwidth,' AI excitedly says.

'Cool. See I told you to have a little faith,' Jaden says.

'I'm beginning to believe a little in this faith and luck thing. But just one percent.'

'One percent is a good start, maybe tomorrow it will be ten percent,' Jaden says.

'Jaden I need you to go to sleep for a couple of hours. I'm going to use some of your neurons to process some of this information coming in. I have to run experiments and tests. You will be semi-conscious as if you took anesthesia before surgery. You can still use a nanoscanner if you want.'

'Cool, it doesn't matter if I'm awake or asleep. I can't do anything tied up to the bed in this straitjacket Superman can't even break out of.'

An hour passes by and Jaden is looking into the clear night sky in a nanoscanner high above the hospital.

'There goes the Andromeda Galaxy and there goes Saturn and Mars,' he says to himself.

He uses the nanoscanner as a low-end telescope to zoom in on stars and planets. The cool night air howls through the scanner and gives Jaden a breath of fresh air. The windmill is cutting through the air creating a cutting sound. The crickets sing in harmony from all directions. A car with bright headlights drives down the main road in front of the hospital. Everything is so quiet and peaceful thirty feet above the building. He spends over an hour stargazing just like he used to do with his father. He comes back into the building and floats by the patient's lounge area where the television is. The lights are out and the television is the only thing lighting up the area. Jaden focuses in on the twenty-five inch flat screen television as a commercial comes on. The aerodynamic shape of this exotic car gets Jaden's full attention.

"The 2019 Bugattee 1st generation Mars Series automobile is the most sophisticated car on the planet. This car is the first to represent the next generation of multi-planet automobiles. This car of the now future has four independent computer controlled wheel motor hybrid engines. Each 301 hp wheel motor is a five bi-cylinder hypercharged engine and they eliminate the need for a transmission and drive train. The four engines total 5,319 pound-feet of torque. This vehicle gets over two hundred miles per gallon of hydrogen gas with its advanced electrical turbine grid systems. This rocket machine does 0-62 in 2.11 seconds on Earth and a top speed between 269-301 mph. That's right ladies and gentlemen, this is the first car that can be driven on another planet. You can take your car in the future with you to another planet. The supercomputer on board this rocket car can adjust to different gravity levels, oxygen levels, atmospheric pressures and carbon dioxide levels…"

'What the hell? Another planet?' He asks. 'That's unbelievable. This car is unbelievable. It looks like it is from another planet.'

"…It has an advanced air vacuum filter system. This vehicle can use a combination of solar cells, water and an advanced electro-nanomaterial polymer battery system in the body of the paint around the car. This new system will allow the car to drive at various lower speeds for months without gas. Around this car's air intake vents are hundreds of mini turbines producing constant electricity for the engines. Two windmill blades on the tail of the vehicle produce a high current of electricity. The suspension, turbine spinning rims and advanced shocks create electricity for the car when it moves and stops. Kinetic energy from the brakes is transferred to the charging system. The car uses gas for hard accelerating and electricity to cruise. The fourth generation run flat tires are made from a nanotube material and synthetic rubber. Badyear says that not even a bullet can put a hole in these tires. Never have to change your tires again. The vehicle also has built in hydraulics for driving off-road or on another planet. The price tag on this planet-hopping car is $2.4 million. We aren't trying to sell this car to everyone on the planet, just the few who can appreciate that the future of cars is here. When man is living on Mars in the next 150 years, your great-great-grandkids can still enjoy this classic vehicle on Mars. We at Bugattee want the world to know the technology is here. This vehicle also has the far-horizon technology built into it. Only 150 were produced and half were already sold..."

'A car that cost 2.4 million dollars? Are they crazy?' Jaden asks.

'Let's see what AI is up too,' Jaden says while he switches his view back inside his body.

His eyes are closed and he can't open them. So much information is coming into his mind from the nanoscanners. He sees five different screens of Internet pages quickly flashing by. He sees pages of: How it Works, Wikipedia, Science for Dummies, advanced calculus, Plasma Fusion for Dummies and 1000 Things about Earth.

'How is it going AI?'

'Very good so far. I went to some classified websites and I'm sure I will get flagged soon.'

'Flagged?'

'Yes, the government monitors how much information an IP address or computer user is getting and what they are looking up. I went to hundreds of sites that can raise a red flag. I learned this from reading blogs. It is just a matter of time before they shut down this connection and start an investigation. Hopefully we will be long gone by then,' AI says.

'Anything interesting or useful?'

'Yes, I must say your species' technology advanced very quickly in such a short amount of time. This new technology called plasma gasification is very advanced technology for a civilization at such a young age. It is a machine that turns any garbage into a high source of energy or electricity. The machine rips electrons from the air and converts the gas into plasma. This creates a field of intense energy like lightning. The plasma disintegrates the molecular bonds in garbage or any material. This type of research I can for your weapons.'

'Awesome, I remember something like that in the movie *Back to the Future Part II*,' Jaden says.

'I've also downloaded very useful information on planet properties, neutrinos, quantum mechanics, quantum tunneling, molecular physics, future nanotechnology, covariant formulation of classical electromagnetism, Lorentz force law, Laplace force, solid-state physics, how the DNS machine works with human minds, an encyclopedia of Earth, gravity forces calculations, and military light reflection materials. I will just need another hour. I've already begun to run different tests.'

All the screens go blank on Jaden's eyes.

'I spoke too soon,' AI says.

Jaden reads WIRELESS SIGNALS LOST, TCPIPV6 CONNECTION OFFLINE.

'Shit, did we get enough information?'

'I don't know yet. I'll have to use what we have. I have to go through hundreds of terabytes of information and run tests in and out of your body. I don't know if it's going to be enough time, it's 1:03 AM now. My synthetic crystal brain and your organic brain are not enough to do all these complex calculations in less than six hours,' AI says.

'Charge the nanoscanners, and keep using my brain to do your calculations. I'll figure out something,' Jaden says in a confident voice.

34TH STREET AND MASSACHUSETTS AVENUE, WASHINGTON , D.C. VICE PRESIDENT'S RESIDENCE 2:17 AM

The phone rings and rings in Robinson's bedroom. He looks at the time and answers the phone while closing his eyes again. He coughs a few times and clears his throat.

"Yeah?" He answers.

"I have the information you were waiting for sir," Peters says over the phone.

"Go ahead."

"The blog came from someone at a New York state psychiatric hospital outside of Albany."

"So, just question everyone there tomorrow morning. Why are you telling me this now?" Robinson asks in a half-awake voice.

"That's not all. Do you remember Jaden Marino?"

"Jaden Marino. Jaden Marino," he repeats, "Jaden Marino?"

"Yes sir, the bi-racial teenager we were after over eighteen years ago, when UFO08 got away."

Robinson opens his eyes and turns on the light.

"Yes, I remember that little bastard. If it is really him, he could be part of this conspiracy taking place. There is a reason why we are up to UFO15 in the past eighteen years, tripling our UFO capture number," he says excitedly.

"There have been over 135 red flags raised at that mental hospital Internet access in the last three hours. Someone has accessed over one hundred thousand websites and over three terabytes of information were downloaded. The FBI reported shutting down the Internet connection there an hour ago. They are sending agents there this morning. Jaden Marino has been put on the government terrorist watch list as a sleeper cell back in 2000. His DNA is also untraceable. They have him in full lock down and watched with a security camera."

"Very good. Let the FBI agent in charge know to escalate this into a high priority. We have to get this son of a bitch and not take any chances. I want to question this man myself. Tell the Feds to go in with full tactical SWATbots and state troopers."

"Yes sir."

ALBANY PSYCHIATRIC HOSPITAL NY 2:45 AM

It is becoming increasingly foggy outside as clouds appear from the west and slowly cover the sky. There is a coyote howling from the woods into the night sky.

'I have a plan AI. Can you get the nanoscanners to use create mechanosynthesis artificial pathways into some of the hospital computer systems here?'

'It is possible. What are you getting at?' AI asks.

'I was thinking we can use the hospital computers to process some of our data. These computers are very fast here.'

'I think that is possible, but the computers have to be on already. I would have to reprogram the nanodrones inside of the nanoscanners to process a computer's CPU similar to artificial neurons created in the brain. That might work,' AI says.

The nanoscanners go out after being fully charged and go into the hospital's computer terminals for inputting patient medication. The computer screens freeze up and become unresponsive. Five computers are processing data coming from Jaden's brain and returning to AI's brain. Jaden uses a nanoscanner to look around the hospital. He finds his clothes and belongings in a locker on the third floor. An hour goes by; Jaden's body disappears for a second and then returns. Light reflecting tests are complete. Jaden is laughing aloud and continues hysterically. Tests continue and energy forces are passing around Jaden's body, which is still strapped onto the bed. A few minutes go by and Jaden continues to laugh out of control.

'I knew you would enjoy watching an instant 150 episodes of *Family Guy*. I downloaded all the episodes for you since I knew you liked *The Simpsons* when you were back on Earth and this television show was similar,' AI says.

'Thanks a lot, that was like getting 150 injections of instant comedy into my veins. *Family Guy* episode 35, *Lethal Weapons* is by far the funniest. So, how is everything else coming along?'

'So far so good. It is a good thing only one person was using the work computer. The data is flowing very well. Your brain is multi-tasking and handling the increased information speeds well. Jaden I'm going to need to use more of your body parts to store weapons energy,' AI says.

'Sure, remove whatever you need, I don't care anymore. Even though I feel a slight headache, just keep going! Just get me out of this hospital!' Jaden pleads.

'I'm going to remove your stomach and small and large intestines. The nanodrones can process any food while still in your throat in a quarter of an inch of space. The remains will be stored

130

inside a sealed storage area made of intestine materials in your ass cheeks. You won't notice or feel any difference.'

'I guess the storage area is connected directly to my asshole right?'

'Exactly.'

Jaden thinks of some jokes and laughs to himself.

'You are full of shit, you asshole. Your ass has shit for brains,' Jaden thinks to himself and chuckles.

'Why are you saying this?' AI asks.

'Well if I knew someone who had their intestines in their ass cheeks that is something I would say to them. I know you don't get it, AI. Just finish changing me into an alien Frankenstein,' Jaden says.

SEPTEMBER 6, 2018 4:50 AM

Jaden's human eyes are closed and he is using a nanoscanner to see inside of the mattress his body is laying on top of. He has animosity towards the little critters feeding on dust and dead human skin cells.

'What are you doing with that army of nanodrones slowly leaving your spinal cord area?' AI asks.

'I'm just borrowing a hundred thousand of them…to attack the alien dust mite colony!" He yells out loud.

A swarm of flying nanodrones spread out in all directions in the mattress and attacks the eight legged microscopic dust mites. The defenseless organisms explode on contact throughout the cushion and spring areas. The nanodrones fires invisible molecule ripping beams at the colonies and they explode on contact. Approximately two thousand green glowing nanodrones spin around the huge nanoscanner like two high-speed spinning compact discs. The nanoscanner resembles a spaceship attacking an alien bug race. Nanodrones are fired towards the dust mites and resemble missiles exploding on contact. There are microscopic explosions all inside of the bed. The bugs try to run and climb through debris.

"I will cleanse this bed's soul!" Jaden yells.

'Jaden, I need those nanodrones to work on your personal shield system. The bugs weren't hurting you, what's the point of this?'

131

'They grossed me out and I know they are there in the back of my mind.'

'You are harming innocent creatures. Remember what you told me about hurting another live creature?' AI asks.

'This is an exception. Anything under two inches doesn't count. This is for all the asthma victims around the world suffering from these little bastards!'

'Two-inch rule?'

"Die you little larva bastards! Die you barefoot pregnant egg laying mother mites. You can't run or hide inside of those dead bodies, I see you. Stop eating those nasty dead human skin cells. Snack on this invisible beam of death and drone missiles!" Jaden yells with a smile on his face. He laughs to himself and it echoes throughout the room.

Ruffo and the nurse watch Jaden on the camera flipping out and yelling to himself.

"Wow, it's only been a few hours and he already snapped. The system works," the nurse tells Ruffo.

Jaden finishes off the colony of dust mites. A half hour passes by and Jaden is watching television in the lounge area through a nanoscanner.

"…Why do you think Professor Brown that America is trying so hard to make it back to the moon first again, if we've already been there six times?"

"I think America is trying to cover up its fictitious landings from 1969-1974…"

"Are you saying you don't believe we landed on the moon forty-five years ago?" The news reporter asks.

"I'm saying MASA's nose has grown as far as it could and now they are trying to get a nose job. If it were that easy to make it to the moon, MASA wouldn't have been wasting billions testing rockets for the past fifteen years. Why not use the rockets from the Apollo program? They worked flawlessly for twelve trips to the moon. MASA has spent over three hundred billion of taxpayers' dollars over the years for a manned moon mission. Why would MASA be competing to beat India and China back to the moon, if they claim they did it forty-five years ago? MASA suffered a huge drawback during the recession in 2015, when its budget was severely slashed by the democratic President. My question to the American public is why are they competing against Japan, China and India to make it to the moon? Are we trying to cover up what we didn't do six times in the early seventies? Are the rocks Japan, China or India brings back to Earth going to look different than the rocks brought back to Earth by MASA?"

'Enough with that moon B.S. Come on, give the USA something under their belt in history. We landed on the moon, Jesus!' Jaden says to AI.

AI is occupied on dozens of other things and doesn't respond. Jaden changes his vision back to the outside of his body as he notices light glowing over him. The camera is showing static interference on the guard's room monitor. They pay it little attention. Ruffo is standing watching cable television in the room at the end of the hall with the full red exoskeleton body suit. Two nanoscanners are still accessing two computers. The other three are running various tests. They are quickly creating a five-foot circle around Jaden's body. A circle of smoke forms around the invisible circle and the nanoscanners quickly go into Jaden's body, up his back and out his right arm. The entire bed jerks and makes a thumping sound.

'What was that?' Jaden asks. 'I felt like I was falling backwards for a second.'

'That was one percent strength of your gravity shock wave weapon discharging from your right arm.'

'Cool. What can I do with my left arm?' He asks.

'Still working on that. It will be something that works with plasma fusion energy waves. I have the energy storage area for your shield system, but I'm still missing a major ingredient. I still have more advanced Andromedian's calculus and science calculations to do. I also need to use another body organ, your gallbladder.'

'Just do it. It is getting close to sunrise. I can see a state trooper car sitting parked outside the hospital's gate. I felt enough of my insides shifting around over the last few hours, I'm sure more can't hurt,' Jaden says.

Jaden is now watching a politician criticize President Paylin on an early morning talk show with a news reporter.

"…I think it was a big mistake for President Paylin to sign the China Open Doors bill, allowing more Chinese people to visit America without a visa, in exchange for lower interest rates on our national debt to them. She is going to open the floodgates of

Chinese people coming over here and not wanting to return home when the bill goes into effect next year. China is nowhere close to the status of Western European countries and should never be given a free pass to enter our country whenever they want. She is literally kissing their ass and making us look weak to the world. A male President would never bend over backwards for China…"

Another hour goes by and the clouds get brighter in the sky. Jaden is back in his body and is looking around the room through his eyes. He sees parts of the walls scraped and destroyed.

'AI tell me something buddy. There are more police cars parked in front of the gates.'

'Two problems, there isn't any sunlight to charge up and I'm still trying to figure out a missing ingredient to get your shield systems operational. A basic body shield is needed for us to get out of this place.'

'What kind of ingredient is missing?' Jaden asks.

'I don't want to bore you with the big words, but I'm missing something that will support the structure of your personal body shield. It would also have to protect you and others from plasma radiation forces and work with electromagnetic energy. The ingredient would also have to be an easy renewable source to recharge when depleted.'

'Okay, keep at it. I'm sure we will figure something out,' Jaden says nervously.

Jaden knows he isn't strong enough to fight an army of police officers. He is building his confidence up, and knows he can get out of this. He continues to monitor the police in front of the gate.

6:46 AM

A silent helicopter flies by overhead. The blades quickly cut the fog around it.

'Oh shit, this isn't good, the FBI are here. There is one robot in the helicopter with SWAT gear on and guns over its robotic hands. There are soldiers in silver exoskeleton suits waiting in a van,' Jaden says.

'You don't have the energy or the weapons yet to fight against this small army,' AI says.

'Listen AI, you said you are missing an ingredient. Let me help you with this problem,' Jaden says while thinking.

134

'Plasma radiation forces and electromagnetic energy?' Jaden asks.

'Yes.'

The helicopter lands on the street outside and agents in all black suits get out. Jaden suddenly thinks back to when he rode Xenos' magnetosphere with Marco in the race. He remembers it protects Earth from the sun's powerful solar flares.

'How about using the magnetosphere around Earth?' Jaden asks.

There is a long pause.

'That might work, but that energy source is too far from us,' AI responds.

'How about using an atomic solar recharge to reach the energy? Then use nanodrones to retrieve the energy. The magnetic energy is constantly coming from the Earth's core right? So it should be all around,' he says, 'The thing Bellona used on Planet 455 when she was fighting all those aliens by herself.'

Jaden thinks back to her body particles going into space where the sunlight was and then returning to the planet.

There is silence as AI calculates this new information.

'That is it! I think that might make it work!' AI yells.

'Cool. How much longer?' Jaden asks.

'I'm done. An atomic solar recharge, or ASR, is when nanoscanners, nanodrones or nanobots molecules are exploded into space from a planet at near the speed of light to recharge its energy from Cosmic rays and other unfiltered particles. In our case, we can program the nanodrones to use unfiltered sunlight and magnetosphere energy. There is also magnetic energy all around constantly coming from Earth's core. Sometimes it takes longer for them to return to the planet, but in our case they can slingshot back to Earth using neutrino particles. Neutrinos are...'

Jaden interrupts, 'Tell me later, let's get out of here first.'

'First we have to do a small ASR, to reach magnetosphere energy molecules and unfiltered sunlight. You will feel a lot of pressure around your body as if you were being squeezed. Nanodrones will be quickly moving around the outside of your body at a high speed, and then the release will take place. A million nanodrones will be released at one eighth the speed of light and then they will return into your body.'

Jaden feels pressure around his body as if he is being crushed by the air around him. A solid invisible force is pressing down on his arms, feet, legs and head. The straitjacket's material is being stripped away. A lot of static is showing up on the camera. The straps holding Jaden to the bed are also being stripped away. Pieces of Jaden's skin are being ripped away from his body. The solid force quickly moving around his body turns grey. Most of the straitjacket over his arms and chest evaporates. He pushes up with his arms still folded on the invisible force similar to an energy shield. Jaden grunts in pain as the clear force field explodes upwards. The straps holding Jaden to the bed are ripped apart along with the straitjacket. The shreds explode in different directions. The powerful energy release destroys the camera's circuits. Jaden stands up from the bed. His eyes read CLOCKWISE ENERGY SHIELD ONLINE 5% ENERGY, GRAVITY SHOCK WAVE ONLINE ENERGY AT 15%, VERIFYING NANOSCANNER'S STABILITY AND STRUCTURE, RECTUM STORAGE CHEEKS 97% FULL, 40% OF BRAIN IN USE, REPAIRING OUTSIDE SKIN CELL TISSUE.

'Jaden, when it returns from space in a few seconds, you are going to feel some pain as...'

'Aggghhhh,' Jaden yells as his body glows. He drops to the floor as he feels the energy going into where his stomach used to be. He fights the pain and ignores it.

'The shield will work the same way you used to control it in the gravity games. Remember your rpm speed you can always monitor from your eyes,' AI says.

Two agents and an officer walk through the front gate.

Jaden stands up and his body feels different than before. A clear invisible shield forms on the right side of his body, then on his left side. They connect together and form two feet around his body as he stands there bare-chested. He admires his more muscular body. He stands there in confidence with his skin being quickly repaired around his body. The shield scrapes the floor. He still has on his hospital pajamas and the diaper. Jaden walks towards the window. He increases the rpm to 2500. The wall and window are slowly ripped away. Sounds of rock crumbling are heard. The dust and debris are sucked into the shield and a hole about eight feet high and five feet wide is created. Jaden can see the outside of the building. Debris continues to fall from the top of the hole. He zooms in on the windmill over 120 feet in front of him slowly spinning, creating electricity for the entire building.

'The drop to the ground is forty-three feet Jaden. Hurry, before the guards come,' AI says.

'I'm not afraid of any guards.'

'What do you mean?'

Jaden concentrates on his right arm as it retracts to his shoulders and the right side of his body leans backwards. His right hand is where his shoulders meet. Nanodrones speed around a fifteen-foot circle quickly moving around his body. He can see white smoke in midair outside the building in front of him. He springs his arm forward and a strong energy impulse leaves it. Jaden releases a fast moving gravity shock wave towards the windmill. A weird swooshing sound is heard in all directions, causing the agents to abruptly stop walking. They look in the direction of the windmill on the rear side of the building. A crashing and metal ripping sound is heard as the spinning rotor dismounts from the long pole supporting it. It goes airborne and continues on a straight path, still slowly spinning. The agents and officers sitting in their vehicles look shocked. All the lights go out in the building. The airborne blade continues on a straight path, then suddenly changes direction straight down and into a school building. Alarms begin going off in the building as backup solar panel batteries start up. The agents run back towards their vehicles.

'Shit, that was cool. Did you see that blade flying and spinning?'

'Jaden, why did you do that, if we can jump down from here to escape?'

'I'm getting my clothes then I'm walking out of this building through the front gate,' he says.

Jaden walk towards the door. The energy shield begins to rip apart the steel molecules in the door. The energy shield goes down to 0.5%.

'That is suicide. Your energy shield is at minimum strength, so is your weapon systems. There are at least ten officers and agents at the gate. You aren't ready to stop bullets yet or other weapons the officers might use.'

'I have confidence I can make it out of here. Where are the nanoscanners?' Jaden asks.

'The nanoscanners are offline for another two minutes. For now, the nanoscanners need a diagnosis anytime an atomic solar recharge is done.'

Sleeping gas is coming from the vents in the building. Smoke fills the hallways throughout the building. The patients in their rooms quickly fall asleep. The white smoke fills the room Jaden is in.

'I can't filter out this sleeping gas. Take some deep breaths and then hold it,' AI says.

He breathes in and out from his lungs, before holding his breath. The pores around his body absorb oxygen. He kicks down the door. There is a solid wall about eight feet away from the door directly across from him. Jaden is blind without his nanoscanners in the thick white smoke that carries a small percentage of tear gas. His screens show that he can hold his breath for nineteen minutes. He steps out of the room and looks around. He hears a mechanical sound to his right. Suddenly a strong hand grabs his body tossing him into the wall across from him. His hands go in front of his face. He has blood on his hands and face.

'I'm trying to enhance your organic eyes for heat sensing.'

'Aww, my eyes are burning and hurting. I'm in pain all over, do something about it,' Jaden pleads.

'That is not working, keep your eyes closed. I'm going to figure out something else. Your shield and weapon systems went offline,' AI says.

"You think you are going somewhere boy?" Ruffo asks in his red exoskeleton bionic suit and helmet covering his face.

'Jaden, something is affecting my ability to perform my duties. Weird energy is being emitted from different parts of your brain. The pain you feel is initiating something,' AI says.

Ruffo kicks Jaden on the floor several times, as he tries to block his chest and face with his hands. The air is knocked out of his lungs. Ruffo quickly punches Jaden in the face three times, as his head goes into the floor breaking his nose and fracturing his skull. Ruffo begins to kick Jaden. Jaden grabs his metal boot and pushes him backwards with all of his strength. Ruffo falls backwards and trips on the cell door laying flat on the floor. Jaden has a fractured wrist, two broken ribs, a swollen face and bruises around his body. He feels the pain, but ignores it. The adrenaline increases around his body. The nanodrones ride his fast moving bloodstream and begin to repair the damage around his body. Ruffo quickly stands up with Jaden.

'Where are the nanoscanners?' Jaden asks.

'They still aren't ready. Some of their structures need to be repaired from the ASR. I'm creating temporary sonar with your ears and senses. Keep your eyes closed. Your muscles are charging and the bone structure in your fists and feet are being enhanced,' AI says.

Jaden ears emit radar signals like a bat. His brain determines the distances and maps out what is around him through the smoke.

"When I'm finished with you, you're going to wake up in the intensive care unit at the hospital, handcuffed to a bed," Ruffo says behind his face shield.

Ruffo charges towards Jaden while he still has his eyes closed. Jaden can see a virtual image of Ruffo coming towards him. The white smoke is making it impossible to see. Jaden feels his muscles bulging as he stands in a karate stance. Ruffo's exoskeleton suit has built in heat sensors. Jaden has a powerful rage inside of him as the pain is translated into anger. AI is having a hard time doing calculations and multi-tasking.

'Jaden, use your energy shield and shock wave weapon system on him.'

'I might need that later. I can take this guy out without that,' Jaden says with confidence.

Ruffo swings his right arm and Jaden blocks the powerful blow with his left arm. He then grabs Ruffo's hard plastic arm, turns and elbows his helmet with his right arm. Ruffo's face turns sideways. Ruffo quickly grabs Jaden's throat with his left bionic hand, lifting him up and squeezing it. Jaden swings to punch Ruffo, but misses. Ruffo slams Jaden into the wall as a strong impulse of electricity comes from Ruffo's hand and into Jaden's body electrocuting him. The built in stun gun sends a powerful jolt into his body. The electricity goes directly into Jaden's abdominal area and the energy is instantly converted into usable energy for his body. The smoke stops coming from the ceiling's vents. Jaden grabs the plastic arm holding his neck. His strength is greatly magnified in his muscles. Ruffo swings to punch Jaden with the other hand. Jaden intercepts it. Jaden struggles with the strong bionic mechanics around Ruffo's body. Jaden grunts and Ruffo grunts in pain. Ruffo releases his grip around Jaden's neck. Ruffo begins to move backwards as he can't believe Jaden is overpowering him. Ruffo's eyes convey his feeling of complete shock.

"What were you saying earlier about your suit being as strong as three men?" Jaden snaps.

Jaden stands up on his own and pushes Ruffo backwards a few steps. Jaden takes two big steps forward and kicks him with a side kick to the chest. A dent isn't made in the hard plastic, but Ruffo falls backwards directly into a steel door. There is a loud thump. The frame around the door is damaged, but the door is still intact.

The smoke begins to be sucked into vents. His nanoscanners go online. Jaden walks up to Ruffo moaning in pain and trying to stand up.

'AI, run that nasty feeling I had when Ruffo spit on me last night.'

'Yeah, that's it,' Jaden says.

Jaden gets very angry as he grabs Ruffo's lower chest and bends in the plastic with his left fingers creating an area to grab. The gravity around Jaden is being disrupted. Jaden lifts him up over his head with his left hand as Ruffo struggles with two hands to break free. He kicks wildly as mechanical sounds are heard. Jaden looks at him through his face shield.

"This is for spitting on me!" Jaden yells.

Jaden retracts his right arm towards the floor and quickly springs it towards Ruffo's body over him. A small gravity shock wave of energy releases from his hand. Ruffo's body flies into the ceiling breaking a pipe. The force from the shock wave keeps his body flat against the ceiling. Jaden tightens a fist as Ruffo yells in pain as his body is being crushed on the ceiling. Debris breaks from the ceiling, but stays afloat with Ruffo's body. His body is being squeezed into the ceiling as he yells in agonizing pain. Seven seconds go by and Ruffo's body quickly falls. Jaden jumps up at the same time with his left fist over his head as Ruffo's body comes down from the high ceiling. His fist breaks the hard glass on the helmet covering Ruffo's face. The punch strikes his nose and mouth causing it to quickly bleed. Ruffo's legs tilt and hit the floor first, then the rest of his body. Ruffo falls flat on his stomach and lays semi-unconscious and moaning in pain.

"Man, I can't believe the RYU uppercut in *Street Fighter* could actually be useful for something in real life," Jaden says while chuckling, "That felt good."

There is a crackling sound in Jaden face as his bones in his nose are being repaired.

'Law enforcement is entering the building,' AI says.

'I'm not done with this asshole yet.'

Jaden lifts Ruffo up by the neck and slams him against the wall at the end of the hallway. His feet are six inches from the floor. Jaden looks him directly in the eyes through the broken glass on the face of the helmet. He hears Ruffo moaning in pain and breathing heavy.

'AI scan his eyes and duplicate the eyes' structure.'

"Who did you say was going to wake up in the ICU?" Jaden asks.

His bionic suit stops working and producing internal air.

"Why are you breathing like Darth Vader, Mr. Tough Guy?" Jaden asks.

"Go to hell, you piece of shit," Ruffo groans.

Jaden increases the grip around Ruffo's neck.

"Look how strong I am? I'm crushing your hard plastic neck with the force of four men."

"Screw you!"

'I'm going to decide now if you're going to hell or wake up in the ICU in a few days, Mr. Ruffo," Jaden says in a deeper voice.

The nanoscanners penetrate Ruffo's brain and go into his subconscious of regret. Nanodrones also access his nanomole. Images of Ruffo's past flashes before Ruffo's eyes and Jaden's eye screen.

"You were bullied as a teenager in school and picked on every day. You threw cats from the roof of your apartment building as a teenager and tortured other animals as an adult. You ran over Bambi on purpose and you tied cows feet together before tipping them." Jaden says.

Millions of Ruffo's brain cells are being destroyed by this forced brain scan as he tries to fight it. Jaden's anger and adrenaline rises again. He can hear his heart beating fast, along with Ruffo's. Jaden finds something of more interest in his memories.

"You had sex several times with your sister's underage daughter?" Jaden asks, "You raped your 13-year-old niece when you were supposed to be watching her? The little girl begged you not to do it and at the time you were twenty-four?"

"No, no, what are you talking about?" Ruffo asks.

Jaden continues, "You felt guilty years later as she grew up hating men and hating herself eventually committing suicide on a drug overdose at seventeen. You destroyed that little girl's life, and then you denied doing anything like this to your own sister, calling your niece a liar?"

Ruffo begins to cry as blood runs down his face. Nanodrones are charging the gravity shock wave energy by creating an eighteen-foot circle around Jaden and Ruffo. Jaden's grip around his neck increases and the plastic can be heard crushing around his neck choking him tighter. Sounds of bones crushing together can be heard.

"I didn't mean to. How did you find out about these things?" Ruffo asks in a low hoarse and gagging voice, while tears run down to his undershirt.

Jaden stares deep into his eyes.

"Please don't kill me," Ruffo pleads while choking to breath.

Jaden releases his grip around Ruffo's neck and he stands on the floor gasping and breathing heavily.

"Thank you, I'm sorry…" Ruffo says while looking at Jaden's eyes turn completely dark. He becomes scared and freaked out by Jaden's eyes turning completely black.

Jaden steps back and pulls down his pants to remove the diaper from under his hospital pants. Ruffo looks at him with confusion.

"Are you going to rape me?" Ruffo asks.

"No, you sick pervert. I'm sure you would like that though. You don't even deserve to be raped in jail."

Jaden walks up to Ruffo and rips off his helmet. The helmet bounces on the floor while pieces of glass breakaway from the helmet and roll in different directions. Jaden places the fully loaded diaper over Ruffo's head and tightens it around his neck.

"I can't breathe! Awwww!" Ruffo yells muffled while he struggles to lift his non-functioning bionic arms towards his head.

"You won't be needing to breathe, where you are going. Remember when I told you if you got in my way I'll kill you?" Jaden asks.

"Please don't kill me. Who are you? I'm sorry," Ruffo asks in a moaning and muffled voice.

"I'm your grim reaper. You don't deserve to be on this planet. You coward child molester rapist!" Jaden yells.

An eighteen-foot circle of smoke can be seen going through walls and around Jaden. He takes a step back and springs his right hand and body forward into Ruffo's chest. The sounds of crushing plastic and metal echoes in all directions. The powerful gravity shock wave's force presses the hard plastic into Ruffo's ribs and vital organs propelling him backwards. The diaper over his head briefly expands as the air is knocked from his body. His body goes through the solid concrete wall and goes airborne. A loud explosion is heard. Concrete debris propels towards Jaden, but his energy shield blocks it. Ruffo's body flies out of the building in a straight trajectory and continues over the front gate area. A helicopter hovering above the state hospital observes the debris flying with Ruffo's body. His body is lifeless as it floats as if it is in space. His body continues to fly in a straight line across the small, two-way street and into a wooded area. Ruffo's body suddenly changes direction and quickly slams into a muddy ground area at three times his body weight. Dirt and mud flies in different directions. The concrete and debris lands over his splattered body with the diaper still attached.

Jaden walks away from the huge hole. His body begins to repairs itself. Law enforcement looks up towards the hole in the building. Agents run across the street to see what landed in the woods.

"He flew 124 feet, not bad. I didn't know shit could fly," Jaden snaps.

'Jaden, officers are by the elevator and some are on the stairway standing by. They are talking to each other by radio.'

'I'm getting my clothes and belongings on the third floor, and then we can get out of here,' Jaden says.

Jaden walks towards the end of the hall that is locked by an all steel gate resembling a jail cell. His energy shield spins around him destroying the molecules in the steel. An arch-shaped hole is created in the metal gate as smoke comes from the edges of the destroyed steel.

'That took 12,000 rpm to destroy. Wish I was in the gravity games now,' Jaden snaps.

There is no one in the security room on the other side of the gate. Jaden walks through it and towards some stairs. Jaden runs down to the third floor and goes through another steel gate. The nanoscanners are watching everything. All the employees are out of the building. A robot with cameras as eyes and guns as hands walks up the stairs to the second floor. The autonomous SWATbot has clothes on like a SWAT team officer.

'Shit my energy is getting very low. Is there enough energy for me to go invisible?' Jaden asks.

'Yes, but I will need to redirect your little shield energy and shock wave energy towards that. The SWATbot has high powered guns,' AI says.

Jaden finds the locker his clothes are in and breaks it open by pulling it hard with his superhuman strength. The locker door makes a loud slamming noise when it hits the floor. He quickly puts on his old Giants jersey, blue baggy jeans and puts his feet in his 1995 Air Jordan sneakers. He quickly tucks his shoelaces into his shoes and runs back towards the stairs.

'These sneakers are feeling very good. So much better than those annoying slippers.'

The SWATbot is coming up the lower stairs and sees Jaden running towards the side of the stairs that goes up. It quickly fires a small tranquilizer dart from its left hand hitting Jaden in the upper shoulder. Jaden quickly pulls it out and tosses it.

"Freeze and identify yourself," the SWATbot says through a built in loudspeaker.

'Now it asks me to freeze?'

Jaden quickly runs up the stairs. The SWATbot runs up the stairs behind him.

'The nanodrones are countering the sedatives entering your bloodstream. I see you are thinking about jumping out the window. I'm increasing the muscle strength in your legs, so you can run faster.'

'Thanks AI. Try to counter the sedatives faster, I'm feeling weaker.'

'It's quickly moving in your nervous system. I have seventy percent of it under control. I'm going to strengthen the skin on your back,' AI says.

The nanodrones quickly begin creating artificial neurons in between the neurons and cells in Jaden's brain. The nanodrones also create artificial connections inside of Jaden's nervous system. His brain usage goes up to sixty-five percent. Jaden can see the robot running up the stairs through the nanoscanners and he can hear the SWAT team officers on the first floor talking by headset to the SWATbot running up the stairs.

"RFID microchip unresponsive in subject. Tranquilizer 1 hit subject in shoulder. Pursuing subject upstairs," SWATbot says through the radio.

"That's affirmative Bot48, subject is needed alive, over," the team leader replies.

Jaden makes it back to the fifth floor, as the SWATbot is ten feet behind him and gaining. The smoke is coming from the pipes again. Jaden quickly runs through the destroyed gate area on the fifth floor. Suddenly everything slows down around Jaden. NANOTIME 100X is displayed on his eye screen. He is running normal speed and everything around him is moving in slow motion. Jaden remembers nanotime from when he was in the Gravhawk back on Earth. His thinking is in regular time. Jaden hears his heart beat once. The SWATbot clears the stairs and sees Jaden in sight. His heart beats another thump. It fires five darts at Jaden and they cruise through the air. His body slowly moves to the left, but two hit his right arm as he turns to clear the gate.

Jaden runs with his eyes closed through the sedative smoke coming from the vents again. He uses a nanoscanner that is directly in front of his organic eyes. He can see perfectly through all the smoke as he holds his breath.

'Run as fast as you can. Your leg muscles are at their maximum enhancement,' AI says.

He runs faster and stretches his legs as far as he can. He sees the light at the end of the hallway. The SWATbot reaches the gate and fires several tranquilizer darts at Jaden. The darts cruise in slow motion behind Jaden. He sees he is running at 16 mph.

'Jaden concentrate on your speed, don't worry about the darts quickly approaching you.'

'But I can dodge the darts,' he says.

'You need to reach 22 mph by the edge of the ledge,' AI says.

'You sure I'm going to land okay, the drop to the ground is about forty-three feet,' Jaden says while he reaches 18 mph and glides over the room door and debris on the floor.

'Don't worry, this will work,' AI says while five darts hit Jaden's back and bounce off his skin.

Jaden hears a very slow talking deep voice on the radio as the SWAT team runs up the stairs to the fourth floor, "Subject is running towards the hole on the south side of the building."

'I feel as if I'm being chased by a Terminator.'

Darts fly by Jaden's ears and three more pass by his stretched out legs. A slow sounding swooshing is heard. The SWATbot is still running behind Jaden, but trailing. Jaden reaches the ledge of the huge hole in the hallway at 23 mph and leaps with all his might. White smoke follows his body as he goes airborne.

'I guess it's time to find out if I can fly like Mike!'

Everything speeds up again around Jaden. The gravity around Jaden's body is disrupted. The light around Jaden's body passes through him. The nanodrones are absorbing the light from one side of his body and reflecting it on the other. This is making Jaden invisible. Jaden's legs are still running in the air as if he is doing a long jump. The SWATbot stops at the end of the hallway as it sees Jaden disappear before its camera eyes. Jaden's body is leaping over the driveway and begins to slowly descend. Jaden sees millions of nanodrones under his feet and around his body quickly spinning around disrupting the gravity. He clears the gate and lands in the street bending down, catching his balance. Law enforcement runs towards the grass outside the hole in the building, looking for Jaden's body.

'Oh shit, I just jumped eighty-four feet from a building window. That was beyond cool. Thank you Air Jordon gods for getting me out of that crazy house,' Jaden says while he takes a deep breath.

A police dog by the entrance to the building is barking towards Jaden in the middle of the street. The police officer holding the dog by the leash doesn't see anything there.

Jaden runs down the street as he passes police cars and unmarked vehicles without anyone in it. Jaden runs up to the last state trooper vehicle. He opens the door, climbs in it and closes the door. He looks on the right side of the steering wheel and doesn't see a keyhole.

'Damn, how do you start this up?' He asks.

'I believe it requires a fingerprint to be started up,' AI suggests.

'Shit.'

Jaden opens the door and continues running down the side of the street invisible. He runs past a roadblock where state troopers are blocking off the street. He turns down another street and continues down the street where cars are making U-turns at. Jaden makes himself visible by thinking about it. His overall brain usage goes back down to thirty percent. He slows down and walks on the sidewalk. Jaden begins to cough and spits on the ground.

'What is this brown nasty stuff I just spit out?'

'That is all the dirt around your body on the outside of your skin. The nanodrones in your skin take all the dirt and bacteria through your body to your throat," AI says.

'Why? That's nasty.'

'You don't have to bath or shower this way. It only happens once a day. The brown liquid also contained the sedatives,' AI says.

'I guess that's cool then.'

Fresh air blows on his face, slowly making his hair move.

'Those idiots are still looking for me on the hospital building property. That was an awesome escape. We need a vehicle to get to the airport.'

'How can we get a vehicle?' AI asks.

'I have an idea,' Jaden says as he watches the cars go by.

'My knuckles are still stronger and my leg muscles are still enhanced?' Jaden asks while looking at his fist and hands.

'Yes,' AI says.

Jaden slowly goes invisible again and runs with the cars on the sidewalk. Most cars are speeding by him. Jaden stretches out his legs more increasing his speed and then he runs in the middle of the street on the double solid yellow lines. Pure oxygen is being absorbed into Jaden's pores and into his bloodstream. He breathes through his lungs as if he is walking. His nanoscanners are checking inside of each car as they approach behind him and pass by. Jaden increases his speed from 19 mph to 25 mph as the last small car in a group drives along side of him. An older white female driver is singing a Fleetwood Mac song on the eighties satellite radio station.

"You can go your own way," she sings in melody.

Jaden swings and breaks her window with his fist. The lady swerves over the road and screams at the top of her lungs. Jaden grabs onto the side of the car as it hits him.

"Damn, lady!" He yells.

She then slams on the brakes and Jaden's body is propelled forward and smacks into the concrete. His body rolls fifteen feet down the street and he lies on his back. She is trying to figure where the voice came from and how her car window was broken. She is shocked and confused. She thinks she hit someone. His clothes are ripped and skin scraped. Jaden, still invisible, quickly gets up and jogs back to her car. He opens her door and she screams when it opens. He reaches over to her and clicks her seat belt. She is confused as she doesn't see anyone and her seat belt flies across her. He pulls her out of the car by her arm and she falls onto the street still screaming. Jaden sits down on the glass in her car and drives off.

"Sorry grandma, I need your car to save the world," Jaden yells out the window.

'That was kinda rough there Jaden.'

'They should make a video game like this,' Jaden snaps.

There is a LCD screen over the air vent that reads: HYBRID ZEBRA BATTERY 109 MILES, GOOJJLE GPS NAVIGATION SCREEN. WHERE TO?

'This little car is running off of electricity, amazing. Car navigation?' He asks.

'It looks like it's an electronic map feature that might be able to tell us how to get to the airport,' AI suggests.

'This thing tells me where I am, this is cool technology.'

He clicks on the GPS screen and quickly figures out how to map himself to the airport.

'I know it looked bad, but she will be okay and is getting help from a passerby,' he says.

The GPS begins to talk through the car speakers, "Good morning, and thank you for using Goojjle navigation system.

Today is September 6th 2018 at 7:30 AM, you are driving northeast on Highway 85. Please drive to the highlighted area on the map screen. Distance to Albany International Airport is 13.5 miles."

'Hey it talks, cool. AI, use the nanoscanners to detect any roadblocks or law enforcement in this path the GPS is telling us to go,' he says.

'Yes sir.'

'Interesting, I was in Delmar, New York all this time. I miss driving,' Jaden says.

He clears out the broken glass still in the window frame. Jaden changes the channel on the satellite radio to the nineties station. Rock and roll is playing. Jaden drives on the highway and AI continues to do calculations needed for Jaden's weapon systems. The sun's rays penetrate the clouds and give the nanoscanners energy.

'How did you know you could steal this car?' AI asks.

'I noticed the posted speed limit was 25 mph here for cars. I know most women drivers always do the exact speed limit. I knew I could run at least 25 mph. I also wanted to get the last car in a pack of cars, so I don't cause a big accident. The funny thing is, something inside of me wanted to throw her out of the car while it was moving. I don't know where these evil urges are coming from.'

'There is a lot of unknown activity going on in your brain, but we can discuss it later," AI says.

WASHINGTON, D.C. WHITE HOUSE 7:35 AM

Robinson picks up the phone.

"What do you mean, he got away?" Robinson asks.

"Yes, sir. There is no trace of him and one security guard is dead," Peters says.

"Dead? Was the subject's RFID microchip activated?" He asks.

"Yes sir it was, but the RFID was in the feces of a diaper wrapped around the security guard's head. The guard flew over 120 feet from the fifth floor. The feces are being sent to the FBI lab to be analyzed. The guard was wearing a generation two full body suit, completely destroyed. Tranquilizer darts were found on the scene and were pulled out by the suspect," Peters says.

"Send me an instant upload of all the surveillance videos. It looks as if this fugitive is still alive and on the run. Set up roadblocks in the area and monitor all transportation places, including the airports. Run the fugitive face recognition program at all transportation depots," Robinson says.

"It was already done sir and the videos are ready to be played on your screen."

"I want to talk to the FBI agent in charge," Robinson says.

"Right away, sir."

...............TO BE CONTINUED.

Written by: Vlane Carter

Creative art director: Vlane Carter

Graphic artist: John Buurman
                 John Moriarty
                 Matthew Garofalo
                 Kwan Wilson

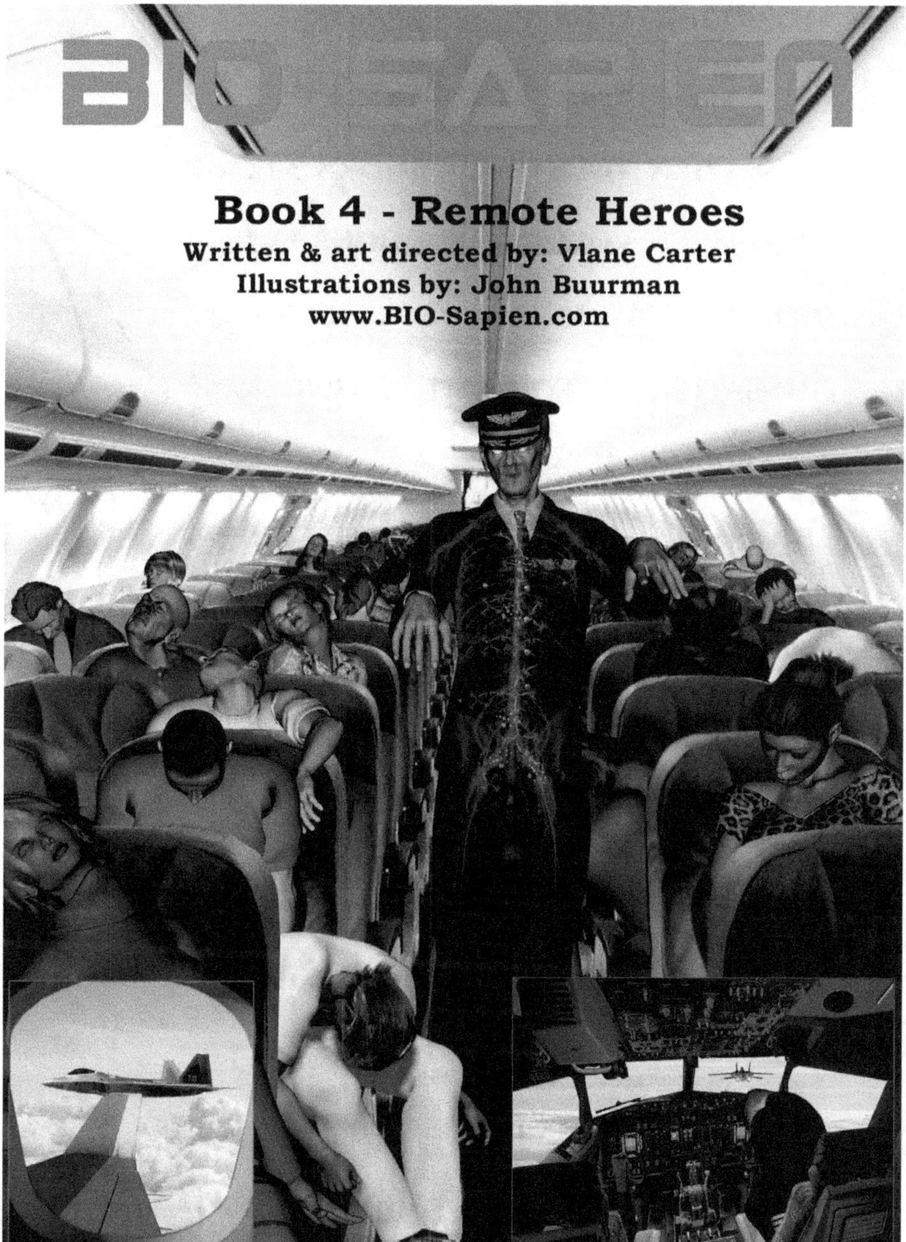
BIO-SAPIEN
Book 4 - Remote Heroes
Written & art directed by: Vlane Carter
Illustrations by: John Buurman
www.BIO-Sapien.com

THE REBIRTH UNIVERSE SERIES:

BIO-SAPIEN VOLUME I BOOKS 1-6

BIO-SAPIEN VOLUME II BOOKS 7-12

BIO-SAPIEN VOLUME III BOOKS 13-18

BIO-SAPIEN COMIC BOOKS ISSUES 1-30

BIO-SAPIEN VIDEO GAME SERIES

<u>BIO-SAPIEN SPINOFF REBIRTH SERIES</u>

BELLONA SERIES BOOKS 1-3

ANDROMEDIAN CHRONICAL SERIES BOOK 1-3
ANDROMEDIAN CHRONICAL COMIC BOOKS 1-5
ANDROMEDIAN CHRONICAL VIDEO GAME
ANDROMEDIAN CHRONICAL CARTOON

BOMANI SERIES BOOK 1-2

MARCO SERIES BOOK 1-2

ROBOGODS & DARCLONIANS BOOK 1-2

TORAGON BOOKS 1-2

QUEEN VALASCA & THE ARACHNOSAPIENS BOOK 1-3

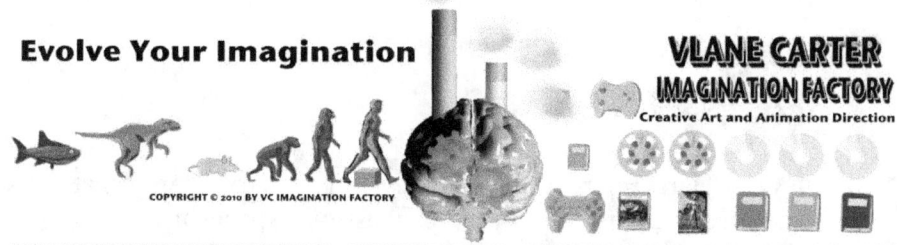

Evolve Your Imagination

VLANE CARTER
IMAGINATION FACTORY
Creative Art and Animation Direction

COPYRIGHT © 2010 BY VC IMAGINATION FACTORY

EQUATION FOR VISIONARY PERFECTION = (PROBLEM SOLVING + OPEN MINDEDNESS + IMAGINATION) X LOGIC^2

VOL I Glossary of Terms

Atoms ripper – Is a molecule destroying energy similar to plasma fusion in the forward shields.

Bioparasites – Darclonians in microbial form. They wait to merge with nanomole to control a human body at high speed. Nanomoles protect bioparasites from human white blood cells. Bioparasites also control armies of microbots.

DEK – Dark Energy Knight.

DEQ – Dark Energy Queen.

DEW – Dark Energy Wraith – Mysterious dark energy that rides like a comet and fuels itself from the exhaust of a spaceship.

DHW – Darclonian Human Walkers. When nanomole and bioparasite merge. Darclonians are controlling human bodies at high speed. Making them super strong and slowly modifying the human body to turn them into super humans.

HBH – Hijacked brain Humans – See positive stage nanomole.

LRSB – Long Range Signal Beacon. It is put on UFOs just in case they get away from the US government. The top-secret technology sends transmissions through subspace.

Microbots – Darclonian robotic or organic organisms that can do a variety of things similar to the Andromedian nanobots and nanodrones. They prepare the human body to become super human.

Molevision – When the nanomoles are in a neutral stage they transmit different visions to other nanomoles when a human is suffering or experiencing pleasure from torturing someone else. It transmits and records dozens of emotions.

Nanoeyes – Invisible to the human eyes, range in size from a millionth to a billionth of an inch. Nanoeyes allow the host to hear and see things at a far distance. It can also pass through most materials. They can be controlled by host or on their own.

Nanoscanner – Invisible to the human eye and range in size between a millionth to a trillionth of an inch. Nanoscanners can do what nanoeyes can, and also analyze materials, scan through objects and determine their structure. They also have other capabilities especially in optic-warp. They can be controlled by host or fly autonomously.

Nanomoles – Are encoded particles sent to Earth over 100,000 years ago by the Darclonians. They sit hidden in the brain of humans. They reproduce in intelligent life from generation to generation, recording everything.

A Nanomole has three stages:

1. Negative - Mole is semi-hibernating and is recording and saving detailed information on the host.
2. Neutral – When the mother ship sends a high power signal to Earth to activate each nanomole in the brain. An 84 hour countdown begins. Humans go unconscious for thirty seconds before waking up, and go back into the negative stage. Some humans randomly go in and out of the neutral stage. The nanomole is expanding and preparing the neurons, axons and chemical messages in the brain to completely take over the human host.
3. Positive – HBH – Hijacked Brain Humans – The nanomole takes control of a human body and walks to upload areas. Bioparasites (Darclonians in microbes) merge with the nanomole and the humans become DHWs.
   * Humans are able to see, feel and hear everything around them, but can't control their own bodies and are prisoners.

Nanodrones – Advanced prototype organic nanobots that were specially made to work with Jaden's body. They work with his body in a collective of different groups and do many tasks.

Nanobots – Metallic, mechanical, microscopic robots that work with Andromedian biomechanical bodies and spaceships.

Optic-warp – The Andromedian species way of traveling through space at a fast rate. The ship approaches a local star at the speed of light, and then the ship breaks down into Quadrillion of molecules and slingshots through subspace at 6-90 second light-years.

Shield technologies –

Clockwise – Forward – 2 layers - First outside layer destroys objects by ripping apart its molecules and atoms. A part of plasma gasification. Second layer protects object or person inside the shield with solid energy force. Powerful projectiles can force through shield systems (gravity x force). The person, depending on the speed it traveled, can feel the force inside. The shield can change into any shape.

Counterclockwise – reverse – 3 Layers – First layer slows projectile and absorbs blast. Second layer gravity matrix analyzes material and stays in one place. It then recycles it into the shield whirlpool, which can be turned into a weapon for firing. Third layer protects objects or person inside with a solid force.

Gravity shockwave – It pulls gravity forces from ground level from all directions and leaves a smoky haze. The object caught in the pathway of the weapon instantly loses its gravity and propels forward at high speed. The object suddenly changes directions towards the ground at 3-4 times its body weight.

TC-100 – An instrument that scans through foreign material. It's like a high powered x-ray scanner that can see inside of aliens and foreign materials.

UF1-retrac team – The UFO police team that specializes in analyzing a
UFO and preparing it for transport to Area 51 for research. They analyze the ship, check for radiation. They work for the government in a special sector and are mostly civilians.

Wraithstalkers – Lightly armed Darclonian ships used for recon missions.

ACTION BURGER RESTAURANTS

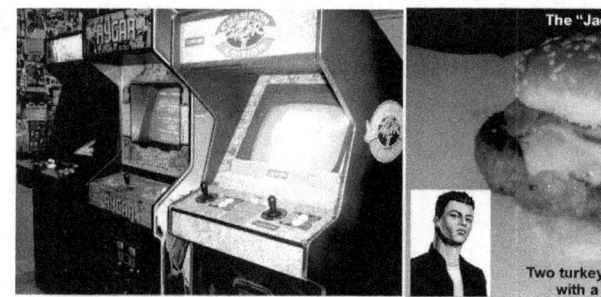

The "Jaden Burger"

Two turkey burgers stuffed with a beef burger.

Comics, video games, good food, action figures, free wi-fi, comic movies & friendly conversation.
Like us on facebook:
http://www.facebook.com/action.burger
Follow us: www.twitter.com/actionburger

www.ingramcontent.com/pod-product-compliance
Lightning Source LLC
Chambersburg PA
CBHW071259130626
46556CB00003B/1388